WINGS

The Journey Home

Elizabeth Emily Hicks

&

William Raymond Hicks

Library of Congress Catalog Card Number:
TXu 1-649-084

ISBN: 978-0-615-42071-4

Cover art & design by Ken Marschall

Published by Inner Realm Enterprises

www.WingsTheJourneyHome.com

Dedicated to all the children,
young and old in our world,
specifically:

**Jennifer, Shannyn, Shane,
Brianna, Jem and Ranen**

&

Dad (David Nelson),
who originally encouraged me to read
Jonathan Livingston Seagull,
and for opening my mind
to all of the possibilities of life…
I love and miss you!

"Why does the thrill of soaring have to begin with the fear of falling?"

~ David McNally, *Even Eagles Need A Push*

Prologue

A breeze carries the first hint of summer, making waves in the pastures far below the granite ledge. Sunbeams dapple the mountain range and farmland as they break through the silver-lined clouds. The ground is ablaze with wildflowers, and the world with the promise of adventures to come. It is a beautiful day to spread their wings....

~ Martha Lee Nelson

FIRST FLIGHT

"There, there, dear, don't be afraid…it's really wonderful! Now Benjamin, watch me. See, all you do is flap your wings and before you know it, you're in the air!" Claire, the mother bald eagle, is giving her three eager, yet wary young babies, their first flying lesson. They are about twelve weeks old and their fluffy gray baby down has given way to their more mature darker feathers. She knows that it is time and they have been excitedly awaiting this day.

They watch their mother with a curious mixture of wonder and anxiety. She is flying, or rather hovering, about three to four feet from the nest, and she expects them to do the same. Each of the young eagles looks at her and then down below their nest, which is nestled in an old gnarled tree, rooted on the ledge of a sheer rock cliff. "You go first!" they each say to one another, "No, you go!"

The eldest of the three eagles, Benjamin, has been looking forward to this day for some time. Now that the day has arrived, however, he is experiencing conflicting emotions. He tentatively sticks his dark brown head out over the edge of the nest with his eyes closed. After a moment of hesitation, he very slowly opens one eyelid and peers down the side of the cliff. He gulps, and looks up nervously at his mother who is urging him to join her. Benjamin knows that his parents and his grandparents before them all conquered this feat, and he trusts his mother completely, but his stomach is filled with butterflies. He understands that he can't remain in the nest for the rest of his life and there is no better time to begin flying than now. Still, that is one far fall!

I could never live with watching other birds flying around me while I look on from this nest, he tells himself. It is this unacceptable thought that moves Benjamin to inch toward his mother and climb up onto the edge of the nest.

Sensing their fear, and yet knowing that this is the natural next step for them, Claire gracefully lands in the nest and says, "No, you go," and with a lighthearted chuckle, she nudges Benjamin forward, away from the safety of the nest and whispers, "and remember to spread your wings!" He glances back at his brother and sister whose eyes are wide with fear and excitement; then takes a deep breath and leaps. Trembling with an instinctual fear of falling, Benjamin forgets for a moment and begins to fall straight toward the ground! Claire is quickly above her son and catches him gently with her talons, while instructing him, "Your wings, sweetheart, spread your wings."

"Oh," says Benjamin, shyly. In a moment, he is gliding. "Wow!" he shouts, as he discovers in an instant the glory of flight.

"Hooray!" "I want to try!" "No, my turn!" announce his brother and sister, Delmar and Dolores, suddenly discovering their courage. In a flurry of wing flapping, they are all airborne.

Claire delights in the knowledge that one of the greatest hurdles of her young children's lives is conquered. They have "first flight" behind them now, and the rest of their magnificent lives ahead of them.

Unexpectedly, a strong gust of wind catches each of the birds and carries them with it. Claire regains her balance and rescues her two younger babies, making sure that they are safely back in the nest. "Well, that's enough flying for you two today," says their mother. "It looks like a storm is coming. Where is Benjamin?" she asks uneasily as she takes off in search of him. "Benjamin!" she shouts.

FORGETTING

Meanwhile, Benjamin continues to struggle against the powerful wind, and is getting very tired trying to return to the nest. He calls to his mother, "Mom!" but his cries are swallowed by the howling wind, which has no intention of releasing him. Frightened and fighting desperately against the strong gale, he is carried far from home.

Benjamin is absolutely terrified by the fact that he has never been away from the nest, let alone this far from it, and with the helpless feeling that he has no idea where he is being taken he begins to panic, frantically flapping his wings to free himself from the wind's grasp. The wind responds in kind and Benjamin is thrown violently against a cliff! Dazed, injured and gasping for air, he falls helplessly.

Tumbling, tossing and turning, he hears a familiar voice in the back of his mind, although he is not quite sure whose it is, *"Your wings, sweetheart, spread your wings!"* Benjamin spreads his wings and regains some balance, but he feels a sharp pain in his left wing. He cannot fully extend it, and he is now spiraling down to Earth, while still being blown mercilessly by the wind!

~~~

Ben falls through a patch of dense fog and lands abruptly in a haystack. A young red rooster walks by and notices something rustling in the hay. Ben pops his head out and sees the rooster staring right back at him. They are both very surprised to see each other. The young rooster is startled and runs to the barn for cover.

Who is this stranger? the rooster thinks to himself, as he tentatively peeks around the protective barn door frame and sees this strange newcomer staring intensely back at him. He quickly ducks his head back inside the barn, and then peeks again and notices the stranger shaking his head and looking around. After a minute or two, curiosity overtakes him and he peers around the corner of the barn door one last time, and, against his better judgment, he says, "Hi, my name is Jeremy. What's yours?"

The young eagle is scared, hurt, and confused, but he relaxes a little with Jeremy's friendly nature. "I...I don't know," replies Ben, realizing that he doesn't remember anything – his name, who he is, nor where he came from. All he knows is that his head and wing are throbbing with pain.

As he looks around, he sees a white picket fence, an old pale yellow house with forest green shutters, a golden retriever dog dozing on the porch of the house, a brick-red barn, some apple, lemon, olive, oak and pine trees, a horse, two cows, several pigs, and this new friend, Jeremy the rooster. The other chickens have run into the barn, frightened by a crack of lightning.

Jeremy is too interested in his new friend and doesn't realize that the storm has come. "Are you okay?" asks Jeremy.

Ben looks at him and then at his left wing and says, "My wing and head hurt...and I don't remember how I got here. Where am I?"

"You are in *Farmer Brown's Chicken Yard!*" Jeremy says, proudly. "We'd better get inside," he adds, suddenly realizing that it has begun to rain, after a large droplet of water explodes on his beak.

An old gray windmill creaks loudly while it spins rapidly near the barn as the wind picks up.

As Ben and Jeremy begin to run into the barn, Ben hears a wild yet familiar shriek far off in the distance. He stops and looks around at the thick pine forest that surrounds the farm, and then follows the young rooster into the barn. He looks back at the stormy sky, still startled from the faraway call.

A white hen and a large adult red rooster approach them, with marked interest. They look at each other and wonder just who this new visitor is. The other chickens start to hesitantly gather around, wondering what Jeremy has gotten himself into this time.

Jeremy sees the concern in their eyes and says, "Mom, Dad, this is...well, uh, my friend. Can he stay with us?" Jeremy's parents instantly size up his unusual-looking companion to determine whether he is a potential threat to the rest of the coop. Jeremy turns to look at Ben. "Your head is bleeding! Mom, his head is bleeding, would you please help him...and he hurt his wing...can you fix it?!" Jeremy asks, intently.

"Well, dear, let me see what I can do," the mother hen clucks and reacts to Ben's injuries. She bandages his head with some hay from the haystack, and begins to make a hay sling for his wing.

Ben is touched by the kindness he receives from Jeremy and Jeremy's mother, and it somehow allows him to remember his name: "Benjamin, m-my name is Ben…"

They all look at each other, surprised by his sudden introduction. "Hello; welcome Ben," Jeremy's mother says. "My name is Etta, and this is my husband, Humphrey…and of course you've met our son, Jeremy." Jeremy's father looks on disapprovingly as his mate tends to Ben. He does not want any trouble in his chicken yard, and he feels uneasy about this new stranger.

Etta showers Ben with questions, "Where on Earth did you come from, Ben? How did you end up in our haystack? Where are your parents?"

"Uh…I…I don't know…everything is a blur," Ben responds blankly.

Lightning flashes and thunder crashes right outside, as heavy rain pelts the roof and sides of the barn. The wind growls as it searches for cracks and any entrance into the barn. The chickens, always unsettled when violent storms come, huddle together and cluck nervously. Ben feels very uncomfortable being in such tight quarters, especially since he has just met these folks. He does his best to settle in near Jeremy and closes his eyes. He continues to hear a call from some distant bird and wonders why it stirs something within him.

SEARCHING

Benjamin's mother is distraught. She had searched for hours for her son. She came home, periodically, to check the nest in case he had returned.

When Benjamin's father, Alexander, returns home from a hunting flight with the evening meal, Claire frantically tells him what happened. Alexander immediately takes off in search of their son.

~~~

Late in the evening Alexander returns, tired and concerned at not having found their son.

"Where could he be?!" Claire cries, desperately.

"Where is Benjamin?" his brother and sister ask.

"I don't know, but we'll find him," Alexander says, putting a wing around his mate and looking on toward their children while extending his other wing to them. "Don't worry, we *will* find him!"

"I should have heeded the wind warnings. Why did I have to choose *today* to start their lessons?" Claire asks with remorse.

"Claire, don't be so hard on yourself," Alexander consoles. "It wasn't your fault. They have been wanting to learn for some time now."

"It just seemed like the perfect day," Claire grieves, feeling inconsolable about losing their boy.

It becomes too dark, gusty and rainy to continue any kind of search, so Benjamin's parents settle in for the night with their two remaining eaglets, but they all find it very difficult to sleep.

The next morning, they awaken very early with the sad realization that Benjamin is still missing. As the two adult eagles prepare for their search, they hear their youngest son, Delmar, say, "We want to come too!"

"Yes, can *we* help?" Dolores asks eagerly.

"We understand that you want to help your brother, but you have many lessons to pass before you're ready to fly so far from home. We may be gone for a while, so please stay here in the nest until we return," Alexander says.

"Delmar and I will wait for Ben to come home. I'm sure he'll be here by the time you get back," Dolores offers optimistically, but deep down she's truly worried about her brother.

Alexander and Claire are both touched by their children's love for their brother and faith in his return.

Benjamin's parents set out in search of their son, flying far and wide and keeping one thought in both of their minds: *He must be alive! He must be safe!* They keep repeating this thought over and over again, not only to bring themselves comfort, but as if this refrain could somehow have the power to actually keep him safe.

~~~

It is late afternoon when, exhausted and despondent, they stop to rest on a high thick tree branch.

"What do you think?" Claire asks her mate.

"Well, there's no telling how far or where the wind might have taken him," Alexander responds. "Hopefully he didn't fight against it."

"Where could he be?" Claire pleads.

"I don't know," Alexander answers, deep in thought.

"I think we should consult with Candor!" Claire finally says with a burst of conviction.

Alexander's response is less enthusiastic than she had hoped, "That spooky old sorcerer! Why would we want to do that?"

"Well that's not very nice, dear! He's been like an uncle to our children. Besides, what if everything we've heard about him is true?" Claire says, beginning to build her case.

"I didn't mean it like that, Claire, but you know I don't believe in anything mystical!" Alexander protests.

"Sweetheart, remember how several years ago he knew that the trout supply would diminish on the west end of the valley toward the sea, and that we would need to start hunting deeper into the mountains? Candor even stayed with the children during some of our expeditions, remember? I don't know how he knew, but folks believe that he has a gift for sight. You have to admit that he did save all of us so much time and effort. I know you were very skeptical, but ultimately he was right!"

Claire continues, "I also heard, recently, that he helped the falcons, David and Phyllis. A hunter shot their daughter, but Candor put something on her wound that expelled the damaging object!" Alexander rolls his eyes. "I know it sounds farfetched, but Alexander, what if there's something to it?" says Claire, begging the question. "Besides, I don't want to rule out anything that could help to bring Benjamin back to us. Perhaps if I had consulted Candor before choosing yesterday to…"

Alexander stops her, "Now Claire, don't start blaming yourself again. These things just happen."

"I'm sorry, dear, I just think that Candor may be able to show us where he is," Claire declares with steadfast resolve.

"Or maybe he'll just send us off on a wild goose chase!" Alexander chides, as he gestures with his wings to symbolize some mysterious hocus-pocus. "We're chasing Benjamin, not wild geese!"

"Very funny, my cynical one!" Claire observes.

"Oh no!" says Alexander. "Don't start with those *'Oh sweetheart, won't you do this just once for me, please?'* eyes," he says reproachfully.

She looks meaningfully at her husband, "I'm really worried about Ben, dear."

Alexander finally surrenders, "Oh all right, we'll go see your silly mystical friend."

The two of them fly off to meet with Candor the Condor. They land on a high craggy ledge located at the mouth of a niche, cut by time into the side of a cliff. From the ledge, Claire and Alexander slowly walk across a wide clearing toward Candor's cave. The old condor has quite a view from his perch – he can see the valley and lake below, and all the way to the far distant sea in the west.

There is a sign next to the cave entrance that states:

Consultations between 11 & 2, Payment: 1 Trout

Claire and Alexander peer into the cozy cave and observe Candor, who is oblivious to their presence, as he is looking through a large basket and tossing various items over his shoulder in a desperate attempt to find…something.

The two eagles glance at each other. Alexander shrugs and steps into the cave, deposits a trout into another basket near the opening, and clears his throat, "Ahem!"

"Oh my!" Candor blurts as he jumps back, clearly startled.

Candor, an old family friend of the eagles, is a large, very odd-looking bird with black feathers and a pink bald head, which turns a bright red when he gets excited. He is a very quirky character, beloved and revered by most for his wisdom, although he has a quality that puts off the more practical birds in the community. Alexander, in particular, does not appreciate that Candor always seems to be mentally somewhere else; as if he has one wing in this world and another in some unseen world, which Alexander doesn't understand and quite frankly can't be bothered with.

That being said, Alexander has to admit that Claire has a point regarding Candor's skills. Somehow, Candor does seem to have an awareness that others don't. How he knows certain things is a mystery, and quite often a source of irritation to Alexander. Nonetheless, their child needs to be found, and Alexander, along with Claire, doesn't want to leave any stone unturned.

Claire steps in with her soothing voice, "Good afternoon, Candor. We hope we haven't disturbed you. Sorry that it's after hours for you, but this is an emergency!"

"Oh, well…" Candor mutters, still a little shaken, "…no, no of course not! Welcome, Claire and Alexander. I was just thinking about the two of you," he says more confidently, as he recovers his composure. He reaches into the basket and smiles triumphantly as he pulls out a scroll, made from old and dried thin bark. "How can I help?" he asks.

"Candor, it's Benjamin!" Claire shares. "He was caught in the first winds of the storm we had yesterday. It was his first day of flying and, well…he's missing."

"Oh dear!" Candor reacts, with a compassionate and understanding tone in his voice. "Well, we do know that there is always a risk when they are first learning. That explains why he has been on my mind so much these past few days," he mutters under his breath.

"Candor, Claire believes that you might be able to know in *some way* where our son is, and if he is safe," Alexander says, somewhat out of his element. He looks away, obviously uncomfortable with asking a mystic for advice.

"It appears, Alexander, that Claire is the only one of the two of you who believes in the power of intuition and the mind," Candor says, wryly.

"Now, Candor!" Alexander replies, defensively. "You and I have discussed this before. You know that I have difficulty with things that I can't see or prove...it just isn't logical!"

"Alexander, tell me this…" begins Candor, "have you ever had the experience of flying along and suddenly you just *know* that far below in the river there is a trout that is so close to the surface it is practically begging you to come and snatch it up? You can't see it yet, but you keep lowering your altitude and then…there…there it is!"

Alexander shifts uneasily, and then admits, "Well of course, that happens quite often; I've never really given it much thought."

"You see, Alexander, you are in touch with much more than that which you see. You know there's a trout before you can see it," Candor goes on, while placing some twigs, assorted herbs and berries onto the crackling fire in the center of the cave.

"I always thought I was just lucky," Alexander says, with a wink to Claire.

"You can call it whatever you like," continues Candor. "My point is that you are connected. *We are all connected…to each other…to everything,* as if by an invisible web, and on a very deep level you know much more than your physical eyes, keen as they are, can see. In fact, you know that your son is alive and safe, don't you?"

Claire quickly glances at Alexander, amazed by the insightful old condor's statement, as an astonishing awareness begins to grow within her. Her attention is drawn to Candor's flickering fire and smoke rising up through a hole in the ceiling of the cave. In her mind's eye, she sees an image of her son appear before her. She can't make out where he is, but she can see that... "Oh dear, his wing is hurt! Oh no!"

Be strong, a comforting inner voice soothes her consciousness. *With time it will heal and be fine, and with the healing will come much discovery.*

The image fades as quickly as it had appeared. Claire consciously snaps back to Candor's cave, and she and Alexander gaze into each other's eyes. "Claire," Alexander says, "I am having a hard time understanding what I just saw...but I believe our son is alive...yet injured. Though something tells me his wing will heal...and he will be fine."

"Oh, Alexander, you saw it too!" Claire replies.

"Yes...I saw something," Alexander admits, deep in thought, "I believe he's alive and we *will* see him again."

"I do too," she responds.

Turning to their wise old host, Claire says warmly, "Oh, Candor, I don't quite know what just happened, but thank you!"

"Thank yourself, my dear. Whatever you were able to see was merely a result of your own belief," counters Candor, modestly.

"Hmmm...well *I* saw it too. What do you have to say about that, old friend?" Alexander interjects.

"Perhaps there is hope for you yet, Alexander!" Candor jests.

They laugh together, although Claire and Alexander are having a difficult time concealing their feelings of worry about Benjamin and his well-being. Candor gently passes the scroll that he has been holding to Claire with his wrinkled old right foot, and says quietly, "Take this with you."

Claire takes the scroll from Candor and replies, "Thank you, Candor. What is it?"

Candor responds, "Open it when you get home. Perhaps it will bring both of you some comfort. Benjamin is such a lively, creative lad, always sketching and spinning tales..." The old condor and eagle couple smile at one another.

~~~

Claire and Alexander fly home and slowly unroll the scroll. They are moved as they look upon it. Claire collapses into the wings of Alexander and they both have a good cry. Dolores and Delmar look on as they too release the burden of some heavy tears for their lost older brother.

WHO AM I?

Back at the farm, several weeks have passed, and Claire and Alexander's dear son is doing his best to adjust to his new "family" and surroundings. The barn is a lofty and spacious building made of very old wood, so it settles, creaks, and groans, and the sounds echo off of the walls, often keeping Ben awake at night. It feels unnerving and unnatural to him, and he thinks the entire structure is going to get blown down by the wind, which is always lurking around, searching for the old barn's weakest parts.

The chickens share the barn with an enormous black horse, a lazy milk cow, several ravenous swine, and some restless, rambunctious pigeons. The pigeons nest high in the rafters where it is warmer and less drafty. At night, Ben can hear them fluttering their feathers to keep warm. Some nights, he will stay up watching them, hoping to catch a glimpse of one of them flying from beam to beam. Mostly, he just sees shadows and cobwebs, where the giant, they call Farmer Brown, cannot reach.

Farmer Brown is a kind, weathered, older man with wiry, graying, sandy blonde hair, faded overalls, and a ragged straw hat. He does a fairly good job of maintaining the farm, but there is a lot of work to do, and there are areas here and there that could use some attention; the roof drips a little when it rains, there are sink holes along the outer walls of the barn, and the fence which encircles the barnyard is in desperate need of paint.

The chicken yard is an extensive dirt area where Farmer Brown regularly scatters grain. The chickens can freely roam around the barn, unless stacks of hay and hay bales impede their movement, but they cannot leave the fenced barnyard. There are hungry things that live beyond the fence, and they would love to get a hold of a chicken or two. Farmer Brown's dog, Ray, is constantly barking and keeping away unwanted visitors from the much larger sheep, cattle, and horses, which *do* live outside the fence in the outlying green pastures. The barnyard has plenty of space for the chickens to get their exercise.

Ben, whose wing is still in a sling, is different from the chickens in several ways. The most obvious is his appearance – he is bigger and a darker brown than the chickens while his neck and underbelly are mottled with white, but his coloring isn't too different from the others at this stage in his development, so he doesn't blatantly stand out. Ben has large, intense eyes, slowly turning from brown to amber the older he gets. He has a long hooked yellow beak with a dark tip, and his sharp talons intimidate the chickens.

As a group, the chickens have decided that they must always keep a lookout for Farmer Brown, and his golden retriever, so that they can quickly hide Ben. They are not sure how he got there, and they definitely do not want to get into any trouble for harboring a stranger. Humphrey has even initiated tutoring for Ben, to teach him to walk, cluck, and behave more like a chicken so that he blends in. All of it feels very awkward for the young eagle, and all the while he can feel his body going through changes.

Ben also has a very healthy appetite, and the grain supplied by the farmer just doesn't satisfy him, so he will find himself hunting grasshoppers and mice when the chickens aren't looking.

Another difference is that Ben is quieter than the others. The chickens constantly want to talk, and anything that crosses their minds flows out of their beaks. Most of them hardly think at all about what they are saying, while some of them have a bad habit of gossiping. They cluck and cluck and cluck about the others, not thinking or caring whether it might hurt someone's feelings.

In addition, Ben cannot help noticing that the chickens are always on edge and tend to frighten easily – the slightest noise sends them scurrying for cover. Ben, however, being of braver stock, often stands in the courtyard and asks the others while they scuttle about, "What is it? What are you so afraid of? I want to see it!" They never have a clear answer for him.

~~~

One day, Jeremy runs past Ben on his way to the barn, and yells, "Hide, Ben! Hide!"

Curious, Ben asks while scanning the area, "Why are you running, Jeremy? What is so frightening that you must hide?"

"Oh, Ben, you should hide too. You must be afraid!" Jeremy squawks nervously without slowing.

"I must?" Ben questions, puzzled, as he slowly follows his friend toward the barn.

"Yes, oh yes! There are so many things to fear," Jeremy calls over his shoulder. "Must I teach you everything?! This is basic survival stuff!" Jeremy admonishes as he hurries inside. Ben follows, though not nearly as quickly as Jeremy and the others.

Once inside the barn, Jeremy settles into the role as a well-intentioned advisor. "Loud noises are the *scariest* and mean something bad is about to happen," Jeremy instructs.

"But where do the noises come from?" asks Ben innocently.

"Oh, we don't wait around to find out!" advises Jeremy.

"Then how do you know...?" Ben begins to ask, but his words are cut short as Jeremy holds up his wing for silence, and then solemnly resumes his lecture, oblivious to any flaws in his logic.

"You must always stay in the barn at night, especially when the moon is full, and you must *never* go near *The Phantom Night Flyer*," Jeremy begins to whisper ominously.

"What is *The Phantom Night Flyer?* Why shouldn't I go near it?" Ben is increasingly more confused, yet intrigued.

"Because it takes our souls to a *netherworld*," replies Jeremy impatiently. He leans in closely and whispers loudly, "You know – *down there!*"

"What? I don't understand. How can he take my soul if I'm still alive? Why should I be afraid?" Ben persists.

"What's a *netherworld*?" he whispers, matching Jeremy's fearful tone. He is uncomfortable crouching and hiding in the corner of the musty, dank barn, and doesn't understand why they have to be there.

"Just trust me...never go near him. My grandfather talked to him for quite some time, and then one day...we found him *dead*," Jeremy says sadly.

Ben doesn't understand his friend's point, but he does feel compassion for him. "I'm sorry, Jeremy...you must miss him."

"I do," Jeremy shares, "...he was so much fun. Grandpa would tell me so many stories of great adventure!" Jeremy continues with gladness returning to his voice as he reflects on distant memories of his grandfather. "He was a very brave rooster, but I overheard my parents talking after he died. Dad was saying that he was very foolish and shouldn't have taken so many risks...like talking to the phantom." The other chickens crowd around and cluck their agreement.

"There are also *mysterious and magical creatures* which come out of the woods, such as *white angels* and *small fairies*. We don't know much about them, but strange and frightening things tend to happen when they arrive."

Ben asks, "What kinds of things?"

"Well," Jeremy explains, "one time a fairy appeared, and not long after that, one of the sheep went missing! It eventually turned up again, but all of its wool was gone!"

"So you think that...?" Ben starts to ask.

Jeremy continues, "And another time, out of nowhere, an angel landed on the roof of the barn just before the wind kicked up and Farmer Brown's weathervane spiraled off the barn roof and almost landed on my mom!" Jeremy's eyes go wide as he remembers, and then adds, "Just to be on the safe side, if you see anything out of the ordinary, it's always best to run into the barn and hide.

"Last but not least," Jeremy says very emphatically, "don't let that scary, slithery *Egg-stealer* catch you!"

"*The Egg-stealer*?! Why? What is it?" asks Ben.

Jeremy jumps up onto an overturned milk bucket, clears his throat, and theatrically begins to recount to Ben a legendary story, in the spookiest voice he can muster:

"*Long ago, on a dark and tragic night, a hen was fatally wounded and dragged off by the Egg-stealer. Now, and as they have done ever since that horrible event, when dusk slowly spreads like a veil across the landscape and the barn begins to darken, the hens leave out an egg, should the killer arrive....*"

Jeremy trails off, solemnly. It was clear that Jeremy, a good storyteller, had practiced this tale many times. The chickens nervously cluck and carry on as Jeremy elicits their fear and excitement. As he concludes, the chickens become quiet as they hang on his last words. Ben just stands there fixated on Jeremy, and in the dead silence one could hear a pin drop....

Ben feels a chill. Finally, he breaks the silence, "Are you okay, Jer'?"

Jeremy replies coldly, "No," his demeanor very distant, as he blankly stares down at the hay, "it hates us chickens!" he says dramatically.

"Why is it afraid?" asks Ben.

Ben's question interrupts Jeremy's trance. "What? Oh, I doubt if it is afraid of anything!" answers Jeremy. The crowd of chickens nods to each other, supporting Jeremy's statement as fact.

"It has to be afraid, if it hates!" Ben comments. Jeremy looks at his young friend, puzzled. Ben is also a little perplexed. He is not quite sure where that statement came from or why he said it, but it felt true.

The wisdom of Ben's statement slowly dawns on Jeremy, and he is surprised to realize that perhaps there is something that *he* can learn from this odd new friend of his.

~~~

That night, Ben falls asleep and is taken into a very vivid and lucid dream. He finds himself in a dimly lit cave, standing next to a blazing fire. Colored stones on the cave walls reflect the flames. The fire mesmerizes Benjamin, and within it he can make out two adult eagles in a wide nest with their baby eagles.

The large adult male eagle lifts up out of the nest and soars away. Benjamin becomes that eagle and he flies down toward an expansive body of water and snatches a fish with his sharp talons. He glides back toward the nest, but before he reaches it he drops the fish and sees the shock on the other eagles' faces, as he and the falling fish spiral dangerously downward to the ground!

Benjamin snaps back to the cave, within his dream, and he is trembling with fear as he thinks about what he just experienced. A very odd-looking, large, old bird appears from behind the fire, startling Benjamin, and says, "What are you too afraid to know?" And then adds, "Go within, Benjamin. Reclaim and own your power!"

~~~

Ben is suddenly awakened from his dream by a loud THUMP! He looks around but cannot see much in the dark. It is very windy outside and pinecones are being flung at the barn willy-nilly. The chickens go on sleeping as the wind licks the walls, and cedar branches scrape against the barn as if trying to get inside. Ben listens intently to the howling, turbulent wind. It seems to him that it has mass, a shape, an ever-changing form. It is alive, intelligent, swarming around the farm as if searching for him. It keeps Ben awake, and he feels that if he were to step outside, the morphing wind would pick him up and send him reeling to some far off place; a part of Ben almost wishes it would.

Stars twinkle brightly through a wide gap between the closed window shutters. Ben stares at the heavens for a long time, while he lies trembling in the hay. He eventually drifts back to sleep, as he ponders his strange dream....

THE CATERPILLAR WHO WOULD NOT BE LUNCH

The next day the smell of wet pine and cedar fills the air, and puddles of water glisten here and there, for it had rained during the night. Ben walks outside and begins pecking at some grain, as he contemplates his dream from the night before. He wonders where dreams come from and if they mean anything. He is having a hard time shaking the images of a dropping fish, falling, and particularly a strange large bird who seems oddly familiar.

As Ben is ruminating over his dream and pecking away at the grain, he sees his reflection in a shallow puddle. His big intense eyes and long beak surprise him. Ben lifts one of his enormous feet and examines his sharp talons. *What kind of chicken am I?* he thinks to himself. He scratches at the damp mud with his sharp claw and traces his hulking shadow. *I am different, that's for sure.* Most of the details of the dream are fading, but he has a vague nagging worry that there's something he should know or remember.

While lost in thought he notices some movement off to his left, near the peeling white fence. A small, plump, light-green caterpillar with black and white stripes is inching its way along the ground. Ben is suddenly aware that he is very hungry. The grain that Farmer Brown had scattered earlier that morning just wasn't doing the trick for his ever-growing appetite.

All of a sudden, the caterpillar stops moving and looks up at Ben and says, "What are *you* looking at?"

"Nothing," says Ben, nonchalantly.

"Don't even *think* about eating me!" exclaims the caterpillar, rather forcefully for a little thing.

Ben responds, "Why not? You look pretty tasty."

"If you eat me, then I won't be able to fulfill my purpose!" the caterpillar counters confidently.

"Really? What is your purpose?" Ben asks, holding back a smile.

"I don't know, exactly, I just feel that it's grand!" replies the tiny caterpillar. "Have you ever had the feeling that you are a part of something really exciting – that something *amazing* is about to happen?" he asks Ben. "You don't know what it is," continues the caterpillar, his eyes drifting upward toward the sky, "but you can hardly wait to find out." He turns back toward Ben. "Your eating me would not fit in well with what awaits me!" he ends with conviction, while glaring directly into Ben's big amber eyes.

This little creature sparks something within Ben; he's glad that he didn't mindlessly eat him. "I think I know what that feels like," admits Ben. "I wouldn't want to prevent you from your grand purpose – and now you've made me curious. You're so small, though...no offense, but what great purpose could you possibly have?"

The caterpillar stands up on a number of his legs and crosses several of his arms, and asks, "Judging by appearances, are you? Is that really how you want to occupy your time?" The caterpillar turns and begins to inch its way toward the fence.

Ben turns away, feeling a little embarrassed. *What kind of purpose could that little green caterpillar have?* he wonders, as he unenthusiastically resumes pecking at the grain on the ground and considers his conversation with the little philosopher he just met.

~~~

Two crows abruptly land on the fence above Ben. One of the crows asks, "What's up, ugly?" The other crow cackles at his friend's insult.

"I'm not ugly!" replies Ben, annoyed. "Get out of here!"

"How do you know you're not ugly?" asks the other crow, enjoying the game.

"I'm just not…please leave me alone!" Ben replies, getting more and more agitated.

"Well, you're ugly for a chicken anyway," adds one of the crows and the other laughingly agrees.

"I'm not even sure that I am a chicken," mumbles Ben.

"Then what are you doing living with chickens?" a crow asks and the other chuckles.

"I don't know…just beat it, okay?!" Ben insists.

"What do you know?" a crow asks. "Yeah, what do you know?" the other repeats.

Impulsively, Ben lets out a loud shriek at the crows and they fly off, completely spooked. Ben's instinctual ferocity frightened them, but they must have the last word. "Okay, then – be alone, you loner freak!" one caws as they fly off.

Ben just stands there watching them disappear into the sky, feeling surprised and embarrassed at having lost his temper like that. The chickens gather around and stare at him, all of them quite worried that Ben may have alerted Farmer Brown. They cluck nervously and scold him about attracting attention to the yard unnecessarily.

"Sorry," Ben apologizes, as he slowly walks into the barn with his head down.

A BARN HALL MEETING

Humphrey immediately calls a Barn Hall Meeting with the chickens to discuss Ben's outburst, as well as the latest developments with the Egg-stealer. Ben is not invited, of course. Feeling more and more like an outsider, he listens in from the confines of the coop, a caged area within the barn. The chickens assemble just inside the barn, while Jeremy keeps a look out for Farmer Brown. They cluck and fuss amongst themselves, as Humphrey struts into the barn, with his beak in the air and his long tail trailing behind. He has called all of the chickens for the gathering and is the last one inside.

He begins, "Order, order, everyone! Everyone quiet down! We have a couple of very important items to discuss! The first topic is the situation with our strange new visitor, Ben."

Ben ducks further behind a hay bale to make sure he is not noticed. It seems less belittling, and he somehow feels like less of an outcast if he can't be seen. He takes a deep breath to try to calm his apprehensive nerves. His eyes wander around the barn, and he observes suspended dust particles slowly dancing around him in the sunlight, which is pouring in through slits in the wall.

Humphrey continues, "I think that he is becoming more of a risk, and that he is jeopardizing our good standing with the giant, Farmer Brown. I propose that he be exiled from our coop!" Ben's heart sinks upon hearing this. Now he *really* feels like an outcast. Jeremy's head drops.

A murmur of clucking erupts among the assembly, and Etta speaks up, "Now, Humphrey, that is very extreme and cold. Ben needs our help and he is Jeremy's friend. I cannot stand behind that decision!" The murmur gets louder.

"ETTA!" Humphrey booms. "I am the leader of this coop and I say he should go!"

"But maybe, given his size, he can help stop the Egg-stealer!" Etta's sister, Fantine, interjects. The other chickens gasp and then fall silent. Ben's eyes go wide upon hearing this.

Humphrey breaks the silence. "Stop the Egg-stealer?! That is preposterous! The Egg-stealer is an evil monster, against which there is no defense. The only reason it hasn't killed all of us is because it wants us to keep making eggs for it!"

"Humphrey is right!" a young hen adds, "and we wouldn't even see it coming. Remember, it killed my sister," the hen adds sadly, "and she was only protecting her egg!" She breaks down and sobs for her lost sister. The other hens gather around to console her.

"There, there, dear," Etta says in a very comforting tone, while placing a wing around the young, grieving hen. "Your sister was very courageous for standing up to the Egg-stealer, and even though she did not deserve to die the way that she did, she is in a much better place now." Fantine and the other hens cluck and nod their agreement. Etta continues, "My father used to tell me that death is like returning *home*. I believe that you will see her again, Laraine."

Laraine stops crying and looks up at Etta while wiping away tears with one of her feathers. "Do you really believe that, Etta?" sniffs Laraine.

"I do," replies Etta, pulling Laraine closer to her. "I really do."

"Even if that is true," another hen clucks, "we still do not want to end up like Laraine's sister!" Once again, the other hens cluck and nod their agreement, getting louder and louder as they weigh the risk of not giving up their eggs against the price of doing so.

"Quiet! The risk *is* far too great! As a matter of fact, there is a new development," Humphrey shouts, as he gestures for one of the hens to share what she heard last night.

A young hen, Jenny, timidly steps forward and clucks, "I heard it whisper last night that it wants more than one egg per visit or else!" The other chickens gasp, and break out into more excited chatter.

"I said QUIET!" booms Humphrey, "I will have order!" The chickens try to quell their noise, but they are clearly terrified.

"What?!" Etta cries out. "Giving up one egg has been difficult enough, and Farmer Brown has scarcely noticed, but a second egg over time would certainly raise an eyebrow. What if he begins checking the eggs more often as a result?"

"Yes!" agrees Fantine. "He would discover the ones being offered up, leaving nothing for the Egg-stealer!"

"This would surely bring wrath down upon us all!" another hen clucks loudly. The noise level begins to rise once more.

"Everyone just calm down!" Humphrey interrupts. "Now let's not get ahead of ourselves! Who says Farmer Brown will notice? Besides, our safety is the primary concern."

"Easy for you to say!" exclaims Etta. "They're not *your* eggs!"

Humphrey is shocked and glares at Etta with a look that could cut iron. "Etta, what did you say to me?" Etta, a good wife, had never challenged him in front of his flock before. It was unthinkable to Humphrey. Etta just storms out of the barn, past Jeremy with tears in her eyes. Humphrey is left fuming, "Etta, get back here! This meeting is not over! They are *my* children too!" The other hens are dumbfounded. Jeremy's heart is pounding as he watches his mother run off. He empathizes with her and the other chickens, but he feels helpless. He looks on past his mother at Farmer Brown's abode.

After a long moment of silence, Fantine chimes in to hopefully cool Humphrey's temper, "Humphrey, my sister is very upset that The Menace has been showing up more frequently these days. We have always had a working relationship with Farmer Brown. We give up some of our eggs to him in exchange for food and shelter. But there is no 'give and take' relationship with The Egg-Stealer – it only takes, and it is weighing more and more heavily upon all of us!"

Ben listens to the passionate discussion and he wants to help, but he is not sure what he can do. The chickens and the Egg-stealer have reached an impasse. *How can I help?* he thinks to himself.

Humphrey takes a deep breath. "Well, for now we give the Egg-stealer what it wants," Humphrey declares authoritatively, as he glances toward the corner of the barn. "We will begin leaving *two eggs per night* for the fiend!" Ben leans back against the barn wall and looks at the corner of the barn, to where Jeremy had told him the egg-stealing demon materializes. Flies are haphazardly buzzing around in the stale air, annoying him. "And…for now…Ben can stay," Humphrey continues, as he looks directly at the area of the coop where Ben is hiding. "But I will not tolerate any more outbursts like the one he made to the crows! Those crows are pests, and bring needless attention to the yard, but we don't need anyone *else* making a stir here. We'll need to increase Ben's chicken etiquette training!" Humphrey finishes and steps past Jeremy making eye contact with his son. Jeremy attempts a smile and then looks down at some straw and kicks it.

Ben breathes a heavy sigh and closes his eyes. *Things are getting interesting,* he thinks to himself. *What happens now?*

THE PHANTOM

That night, as the chickens finally settle down to sleep, Ben becomes increasingly restless, so he decides to take a walk. He waits for all of the chickens to fall asleep so that he can leave the coop, which is of course "against the rules." Silvery moonbeams pass through slits in the barn walls, casting eerie shadows throughout the barn. A shadow quickly moves behind Ben and he glances to look back, but sees nothing except the two eggs left out near the corner of the barn for the Egg-stealer. The eggs – and the neatly stacked hay upon which the hens carefully placed them – are shrouded in moonlight.

Ben sneaks toward the barn entrance, doing his best to avoid stepping on strands of crisp hay so as not to awaken the chickens and get into trouble. Farmer Brown's gigantic black horse is awake and staring directly at Ben. It snorts and loudly stomps its massive hoof as Ben walks by. Ben stops suddenly and, after hesitating a moment, he looks around and then cautiously and quietly creeps outside of the barn into the cool, crisp night air, where bats, moths and fireflies fly about. Other night creatures and wild beasts roam around in the nearby dark and misty woods. Yellow eyes peer back at Ben from beyond the fence, as crickets and frogs create a bewitching melody.

He is lost in thought. Although the chicken coop is a cozy home within the barn, it feels confining for Ben, particularly tonight, given the emotionally heated day everyone had. He is feeling more and more frustrated by the growing sense that something isn't right, almost as if he is somehow bigger than his body. He feels as if he might burst if he doesn't *do* something, but he doesn't know what he should or can do!

Ben is beginning to accept that he is a chicken, for his life with them is all that he can remember. He doesn't *feel* much like a chicken, though, and he definitely doesn't seem to fit in with the rest of them. Ben's weeks in the chicken yard are taking a toll on his well-being. He feels clumsy and slow because he doesn't run for cover as quickly and as instinctively as the rest of the chickens, which causes more dark looks from Humphrey, who now watches him constantly. When the others are busily clucking about this or that, he often finds himself looking up at the birds of the air. He watches them soar high above the ground, and then he closes his eyes and imagines what it must be like to be so majestic and free.

Ben recalls an afternoon in his recent past when he was standing alone in the middle of the chicken yard, gazing up at some wispy clouds.

~~~

"What do you think, Ben?" Jeremy asked.

"Huh? Uh...wha...? What do I think about what?" Ben said, slightly startled. He had been drifting on a lovely warm thermal air pocket in his mind and his young friend's question brought him quickly back to the ground.

Jeremy laughed at his friend's obvious disorientation. "You were daydreaming about flying again, weren't you? Oh, Ben, you're so funny! Don't you know that chickens can't fly? They just aren't meant to. That's just the way it is," Jeremy stated very matter-of-factly, repeating word for word his father's sage and sobering advice.

"But Jeremy, I don't always feel like a chicken," Ben confessed.

"Well you are, and the sooner you accept it the happier you'll be!" Jeremy snapped.

"Really?" persisted Ben. "I'd like to be happy, but the thought of having to stay on the ground for the rest of my life doesn't seem to be much comfort."

"Trying or wishing to be something you're not doesn't seem to be too practical," preached Jeremy. "What's the matter with being a chicken anyway?" Jeremy added, defensively.

"Oh, nothing, I suppose," Ben said wistfully as he looked up at a pair of eagles soaring overhead. "What do you think about the other birds, Jeremy, the ones that can fly? Do you ever wish you could? Fly, I mean?" asked Ben.

"I don't really think about it much. I think it would be really scary being that far from the ground," Jeremy replied, his eyes going wide at the thought of it. "I'm very happy down here on the ground, thank you very much!" he added.

"Oh, but to fly…just imagine how much you could see!" Ben said with an air of adventure, looking back up at the pair of eagles, his eyes flashing with excitement. Jeremy just looked at him blankly, shook his head and then began to peck at a bit of grain on the ground....

~~~

A wolf howls in the distance, and Ben's mind returns to the present moment. Ray, the farmer's golden retriever, awakens and barks at some unseen intruder. Wandering beyond the barn under the clear moonlit sky, Ben is now left alone with his thoughts and dreams, and is wondering what he would be if he could be anything. He is feeling a little wild in his heart as he takes in the sights, sounds and scents of the seductive night. *Maybe Jeremy is right*, the young eagle considers. *Perhaps I should just accept that I am a chicken and stop wasting my time daydreaming about being something else – it only seems to lead to frustration and disappointment anyway. I could be happy here with the chickens and just make the most of it.* Ben does his best to feel content that he has come to a decision about how to live.

"*Who, who, who are you?*" a haunting voice asks, startling Ben. Ben looks up to see a dark figure fly overhead, temporarily blocking out the light from the full moon.

A sudden feeling of dread comes over Ben as he recalls the warning from Jeremy about The Night Flyer. "A-a-are you the phantom who takes our souls to the other side?" Ben asks with trepidation.

"Now, what in the world would I do with your soul? That's silly! I am no phantom; I'm a *barn owl!*" says the owl scornfully, indignantly, and with a chuckle. The moon now clearly illuminates the owl, perched upon a branch of a large pine tree. "My name is Aloysius," declares the owl. "Who, who, who are you?" he asks again with a smile in his voice.

"I-I don't know! I mean my name is Ben; I guess I'm a chicken, but I don't *feel* like a chicken...I'm not like the others," he says woefully.

"Then why do you think you're a chicken?" asks the owl with a growing sense of amusement.

"Well, I live with them, and all I know is this barn. I don't remember anything else, but sometimes I feel like there's something I should remember, or be, or do, or...oh, I don't know..." Ben says, crestfallen. "I feel as if no one understands me...they all think I'm weird. I don't think the way the others do, or act the way they do, or even like the things they eat!"

"What would you prefer to eat...mice?" the owl asks, wryly.

"Yes! How do you know?" Ben says, surprised and a little embarrassed by the owl's question. "I just feel like I don't belong!" he finishes with a heavy sigh.

"*Belong?*" asks the owl.

"You know, fit in like everyone else," Ben explains.

"Do you *want* to fit in? Do you want to cluck and fuss and gossip, and run and hide the minute things get interesting? Is *that* who you are? *What do you feel deep down inside yourself?* Who, who, who do you want to be?" prods the owl.

"I can be who I *want* to be?" Ben asks with tentative hopefulness.

"Of course!" replies the enigmatic guide.

"What do you mean, *of course*?! I can't *fly*. All I want is to fly!" the young eagle admits, looking up at the sky with a subdued longing.

"Oh dear, this one has been with the chickens too long!" the mysterious old owl mutters to himself, and then says to Ben, "All you want is to fly? Then fly!"

"I can't, I'm a *chicken*!" Ben utters, automatically. He then sighs and looks down at his sling.

The owl smiles, and shares, "Just because a thought pops into your head, you don't need to make it real by thinking about it. Who's in control of your mind? Young one…whether you think you can or think you cannot, either way, you are correct."

"I can…or can't? What do you mean?" Ben asks, impatiently.

"Be careful, young Ben," continues Aloysius, "for what you believe you will achieve, if you focus enough upon it. Whatever you find yourself focusing on, you will attract into your life. You are torn between two primary thoughts. You want to fit in and be accepted by your new family, the chickens, and you are also being called to be who you are in the fullest and richest way! 'I can't fly,' you say! Tsk, tsk, tsk! You are beginning to think like a chicken! What do you want more than anything?" the wise owl asks, almost harshly, yet there is an unmistakably caring tone in his voice.

As if it were too much to hope for, Ben declares, "*I want to fly!*"

"Do you think you would have a desire so compelling without the means to fulfill it?" asks the owl patiently.

"It doesn't make sense that I would," Ben admits, thoughtfully, "…unless the world just isn't fair."

"It's only unfair if you compare," shares the owl. "Look inside your heart and let it tell you who you are and why you are here. What if you kept your mind and thoughts on what you want rather than what you don't want? There is a law of nature that very few are aware of because it is not as obvious as the one that pulls things to the ground. It can be very subtle and requires patient observation over time to notice its effects, but once you experience it, your life will never be the same."

"What is this law?" asks Ben, intrigued.

"Like the one keeping you on the ground, this one is invisible to the eyes, and yet its source is not coming from the Earth...but from you!" replies Aloysius.

"From me?!" blurts Ben, astounded by this last statement.

"Your mind to be exact," clarifies the owl. "Just as the earth you are standing on is pulling you toward it, so the thoughts and images you hold in your mind are attracting like things to them. This is why you need to become the master of your mind."

"But how did I end up here?" inquires Ben. "Did I imagine this place?"

"Only you can answer that, young one," the owl responds, "but I do know that a law is a law and it does not make exceptions. Just notice...and you will find that this is the case."

"Wow...but everything seems so...I don't know...so random," comments Ben while holding up his good wing and pointing out all of the insects flying around.

"Appearances are deceiving...*do not be fooled!*" warns Aloysius. "Close your eyes, quiet your mind, and you will see that there is a delicate order and grace to everything, that you – and all of us – have the ability to tap into, and therefore shape our lives. It's our choice…or let the *winds* take us where they will…."

Ben closes his eyes, and in the enchanting night air he *does* feel a sublime peace. He has a brief memory of being in a…a nest…and etching something…but the memory is quickly replaced by other fleeting thoughts….

"Who, who, who are you?" chants the wise old teacher.

Who am I? Ben asks himself in the silence. After a few moments, Ben opens his eyes and his mysterious visitor is gone. Standing alone in the moonlight, he gazes up at the empty branch upon which his sage visitor had just been perched. *Did that just happen? Did a…barn owl…just suggest that I have access to some power to create my life the way I want it…that I could actually… fly?* Ben ponders incredulously. *How could that be?*

His mind is racing with thoughts and questions as he walks back to the barn, *Who was he? Should I know him? I sure wish I could remember my life before this place!* Ben kicks a pinecone and carefully slips back inside the barn, and notices that the eggs left out for the Egg-stealer are *gone*!

~~~

Days slip by as Ben thinks about what the owl had said to him. He imagines what it would be like if he could actually fly, like a barn owl, maybe. He also remembers the bold, little green caterpillar, wondering what his "grand purpose" could be, as the tiny creature crawls along the top of the fence, munching away on some leaves that are touching the fence. For days Ben is lost in thought, "Who, who, who are you?" echoing in his mind.

From that evening on, whenever he gets the chance, Ben finds himself now and again climbing up on top of a pile of hay bales, which are stacked behind the barn somewhat like a stepped pyramid. He knows that he is rebelling against 'the order to blend in,' but his heart feels called. At first, he climbs with apprehension from one step to the next, nervously navigating his way while trying not to look down, in order to reach the top stack where he can look around from a higher perspective. Over time, however, Ben becomes more and more confident, easily jumping from one step to the other all the way to the top. His wing is feeling better and better with each passing day and he is feeling more powerful.

This stack of hay bales is where he likes to go when he wants to be alone. Ben can sit up there for hours, affirming to himself that he can fly, feeling the warmth of the sun on his feathers. He pictures himself in his mind's eye soaring over the adjacent green pasture and nearby trees. From his own personal "mountain," Ben can look out over the fence at grazing farm animals, rabbits, and various beasts which step out of the woods, watching him with suspicion. Upon seeing some of these animals, Ben feels hungry, so when he spots a mouse searching for food near the barn, he hops down and gobbles it up.

Jeremy looks up at Ben one sunny day and shouts, "What are you doing up there, Ben? Come down from there this instant before you hurt your other wing...or worse!" he demands, as if he were Ben's mother.

Ben looks at Jeremy for a moment, annoyed that Jeremy is treating him like a child. "I like it up here!" declares Ben. "It feels right. You should try it, Jeremy."

"No way!" Jeremy protests. "Are you kidding? The milk bucket is as far from the ground as I want to be."

"Suit yourself!" says Ben.

"Hey look!" comments a passing crow. "Ben thinks he's like one of us!"

The crow's companion turns to look at Ben, who is sitting high on the hay. It just shakes its head as they keep flying. "What a weird bird," it mutters.

Ben shrugs and hops from one bale to the next with the greatest of ease, astonishing Jeremy in the process. He reaches the ground next to Jeremy with a big grin and a *"Ta da!"* as he bows and spreads his good wing outward.

"You really are a very bizarre chicken, Ben, that's for sure. Don't let my mom catch you up there," clucks Jeremy, "or worse, my *dad!*"

Ben only smiles in reply, and he struts with Jeremy into the barn, where the two of them begin to play and draw images in the dirt floor of various animals. They point out each animal's uniqueness. At one point, Ben decides to imitate the milk cow and those annoying crows, which causes Jeremy to fall onto some straw and laugh at his friend's ridiculous display. The milk cow, however, is not amused as it chews on some hay and stares blankly at Ben.

THE COUNCIL

Meanwhile, Ben's parents are doing their best to cope with the fact that he is lost to them. They do everything they can to carry on with their lives, all the while feeling the hole that Benjamin used to fill. He was always an adventurous and creative soul, who loved to play act and carve on sticks, leaves, and bark from the nest – whatever he could get his claws on.

One day, when Alexander is off hunting for the family and Claire is tidying up their nest, she comes across some twigs that Benjamin had been carving on and she feels a lump forming in her throat. She thinks back to Benjamin's first peck through his shell, his first cry, his first bite of trout, his first wobbly stand and small shaky step, and his very first words. Her mind drifts back to one particular evening….

~~~

Alexander is feeding Benjamin who got so excited while eating that he almost choked! "When I can fly, I'll be the fastest, strongest and bravest eagle ever…you'll see!" Benjamin proclaims.

Claire began to laugh, and Alexander glanced at his mate with exasperation. Claire lightheartedly says, "Benjamin! You may eat or speak, but not both at the same time! We have no doubt that you'll be the fastest and bravest eagle that's ever flown in our skies, but until then, it won't do for you to choke on your dinner!"

"I will! You'll see!" Benjamin said while excitedly gulping down bites of trout....

~~~

A shriek off in the distance interrupts Claire's reverie. She turns her thoughts and attention to the task at hand: getting the nest prepared for Alexander's return with dinner for their family. She wonders how this nightmare could have happened.

She sees her husband flying toward them. *He's magnificent*, she thinks to herself, as she watches him approach their nest. Losing Ben has taken its toll on all of them, but Alexander has kept his focus on the fact that meals still need to be caught, though none of them have fully regained their appetites.

As he lands with a large trout she smiles at him, but he can see that she is still struggling. "Have you heard anything? Has Candor anything to report?" he asks.

"No, nothing yet...well, just that he has assembled a team that he is very excited about. He has called a meeting of The Council for tomorrow," Claire says with lackluster.

"We have to be patient, Claire. Remember how brave our son is," Alexander says, doing his best to boost her spirits.

"I know," she says, wiping away a tear. "I'm trying to have faith and trust my inner knowing that tells me he's on the adventure he's always dreamt of. It's just so difficult, not knowing for sure…not seeing him."

Alexander puts his wing around her and looks on toward their younger son and daughter who have been equally saddened by the loss of their big brother. They all solemnly eat their evening meal and settle in for the night.

~~~

The next day, a gathering assembles on the ledge near Candor's cave. Quite an assortment of friends has flown far and wide to lend their support to the eagle family.

Candor calls the meeting to order. "Thank you everyone for your presence here today. I know that it means so much to our eagle friends, Claire and Alexander, that you have taken this mission to heart. We have a lot to update everyone on since our last meeting. Benjamin has been located, and while we know that he is safe, it seems that he is having difficulty remembering who he is, and with a wounded wing, well, there is no telling how long he will be grounded!"

A murmur goes through the crowd. Claire and Alexander give each other hopeful glances. "He's been found?!" Claire reacts with a sudden burst of excitement.

"Where is he?" adds Alexander, moving toward Candor.

"How can we help?" a young enthusiastic sparrow chirps.

"Well, time will have to be our partner in healing his wing, but our greater concern is that he is beginning to take on the limiting beliefs of his hosts. While they seem to mean well and are apparently doing their best to care for him as one of their own…that is precisely the problem! They are superstitious groundlings – chickens to be exact – and know nothing of our ways. We are assembling a small team to keep an eye on him and inspire him to remember who he is, when the time comes. We must trust that his wing will heal completely and he'll be able to rejoin us. For now, though, it is critical that he remain where he is and heal fully. We can't afford to have him re-injure himself before he is ready to resume flying."

Claire and Alexander quickly glance at each other and Claire asks, "But what if his wing doesn't heal?"

"Let's not focus on that…there's no value in entertaining an idea that only brings fruitless pain," Candor says solemnly. "We must trust that he is whole and complete, and know that with time he will discover his wings again. The best thing that we can do is to envision him flying as he was born to do. In the meantime, discretion is very important! Most of you can easily check in and even converse with him. Our friend, Aloysius, had a very informative meeting with him, and much of this update comes from what he gathered."

Candor turns toward the eagle couple and states earnestly, "Claire and Alexander, I know that you must want to reach out to him, but it is very important that you do not try to contact him. Benjamin must regain himself on his own, and in his own time. Until he is ready to fly again, it could be too frustrating and overwhelming for him to see you. Also, the human could become alarmed if he sees a pair of eagles getting too close to his chickens."

Alexander clears his throat to speak, but Candor continues, "Alexander, please trust me, it would not be safe for you, nor Benjamin. Apparently, the chickens are hiding him from the farmer. Fortunately, you and Claire have extremely sharp vision and can see him clearly over a long distance. I think, for now, it would be in everyone's best interest for you both to observe him from a higher vantage point. We must respect that this is a journey that Benjamin has chosen." Candor observes Alexander about to speak and holds up his wing to silence him. "As difficult as it is to witness, and as tempting as it may be to tell him who he is, we must honor his path of self awakening. Who are we to say what his path holds for him? Gentle nudges and questions can be great ways to inspire his inquiry and discovery without causing him to withdraw and resist. We can all be of assistance to Benjamin. I know all of you will do your best to help him grow. Now, let us hear from those who have observed him…."

The meeting goes on for a while longer, while those who have seen him report kindly to Claire and Alexander, who both take in any and all information about their beloved son. When the meeting is over, Candor thanks everyone and moves mysteriously back into his cave.

~~~

Claire feels conflicting emotions. Her son is alive and they know where he is, but she can't speak to him! How can she possibly go about her days without attempting contact with Benjamin? Alexander is absolutely furious! He does not like being told what he should or shouldn't do…especially by Candor!

Claire, who has been holding the scroll given to them by Candor, passes it to Alexander. He relaxes a little and nods affirmatively to Claire, while wrestling with a mixture of emotions, and says, "I am doing my best to believe Benjamin will be fine."

He embraces Claire and they both turn to look off to the southwest toward the farm, sending their son loving thoughts for his quick recovery.

A FAIRY

Ben often watches the caterpillar's movements, ever since the day they had spoken. He feels a connection to this strange little friend. Today he notices it hanging vertically from the fence crossbeam. The caterpillar mysteriously begins to manifest silk, and is methodically covering itself with it. Ben wonders what odd thing the little creature is up to now?

"What in the world are you doing, little friend?" Ben asks.

"I'm not really sure," responds the caterpillar.

"Didn't your parents tell you what to expect?" inquires Ben.

"I have never known my parents," shares the little creature. "I was abandoned at birth."

"Oh, I'm sorry," Ben consoles. "I can relate. I can't remember my parents either." Ben continues, "It looks like you're wrapping yourself up, but how can that possibly lead you closer to your grand purpose? It looks like you're closing yourself off from the rest of the world."

The caterpillar pauses and looks down at Ben, confessing, "I feel that I'm changing, but I don't know what I'm changing into. I have no idea what the future holds. I feel out of control…and there's nothing that I can do about it. I just feel compelled to do this…but I'm afraid!"

Ben is a little surprised by his friend's confession since he has always seen the caterpillar as pretty sure of itself. Wanting to be supportive, Ben says, "I'm sure you'll be fine. I guess you just need to trust the process." Ben felt a little out of his element coaching the caterpillar, but it seemed like the thing to do.

"Thanks, friend," says the striped caterpillar, warmly. "I needed to hear that." He resumes building his cocoon as Ben looks on, secretly concerned for the little one.

"By the way," Ben adds, "I'm sorry for judging you before. I don't like to be judged by my appearances either...it doesn't feel good."

"Oh...that's okay," the caterpillar replies while continuing to spin silk. "I'm just happy you didn't eat me!" It smiles and looks at Ben, and they both have a good laugh together.

"Good luck with your grand purpose, my friend," Ben says.

Ben turns his eyes upward to some billowy white clouds and thinks about what *his* grand purpose might be.

Jeremy runs by and asks, "What are you doing, Ben?" as he jumps into a haystack.

"Oh, nothing," replies Ben.

"Then you'd better hide!" Jeremy whispers from beneath the hay. "The cute young hens and I are playing hide and seek. You don't want them to find you!"

"I'm not up for playing today, Jer'," Ben says.

"You're it!" shouts Jenny, as she tags Ben with one of her wings and runs away.

"I'm not playing!" Ben calls after her.

She stops and turns around, asking, "You're not much of a hider these days, are you, Ben?"

"No, I guess not. I have a lot on my mind," he replies.

"Well, you'd better start practicing," Jenny advises. "You want to be sharp in case the Egg-stealer comes after you!" She lunges at Ben with her wings, trying to scare him, but Ben doesn't flinch.

"Fine," she says, "but don't say I didn't warn you. Where is that charming friend of yours?"

"Aaarrrgh!" Jeremy jumps out of the hay to scare her.

"Aaahhh! It's the Egg-stealer!" she screams and runs off.

Jeremy laughs and rolls in the hay, "I showed her, didn't I, Ben?"

"Uh, yeah, you sure did," Ben replies, halfheartedly.

Jeremy climbs out of the hay and walks over to Ben while shaking and picking off hay from his feathers. "What's up, Ben?" he asks.

Ben looks through the fence at a family of squirrels and says, "Jeremy, I can't stop thinking about that Egg-stealer taking our eggs. I wonder if anybody else is afraid of it. Those squirrels don't seem to have a care in the world!"

Jeremy responds, "Those squirrels are different – they're wild gatherers, while we are civilized chickens. Besides, some of the hens even think that the Egg-stealer is protecting us from even greater terrors!"

"I know…I've overheard that theory discussed at a recent Barn Hall Meeting as well. Do you really believe that the Egg-stealer is protecting us?" Ben inquires.

"I don't know, but there are all kinds of dark forces lurking about. All I know is that ever since we've been giving up our eggs, we haven't lost anyone," Jeremy says trying to justify the chickens' dilemma.

"You've lost your future children!" Ben shrieks.

Jeremy is stunned by his friend's passionate outburst. "Ben! Are you *trying* to get yourself expelled from the coop?!" he reacts, looking around. He doesn't want to attract his father's wrath again, nor does he want to think about this anymore. "Do we always have to talk about the Egg-stealer? I just wish it would go away!" Jeremy turns away from his friend, feeling helpless and frustrated by the whole subject. He looks through the fence and says, "Let's talk about those squirrels. What do you think they're doing with that acorn?"

Ben takes a deep breath, realizing that this topic is disturbing to both of them. He turns to look through the fence and notices that instead of the usual gathering of acorns that he has often seen the squirrels doing, today they seem to be running with an acorn, back and forth, playing keep away. One team is trying to keep the acorn away from another team, throwing and tossing it to each other. "It appears to be a game," Ben observes.

Ben and Jeremy watch for hours as the squirrels run past the opposing team members with the acorn. One squirrel with the acorn reaches a particular goal area, and he throws the acorn to the ground, doing a cute little victory dance when he scores. All of his teammates cheer and jump up and down. They have a great time playing "acornball," as Jeremy and Ben call it. They enjoy watching the squirrels play but Ben feels uneasy. It seems to him that he should be as happy and carefree as the squirrels, but all he can think about is the Egg-stealer…and, of course, flying.

He comments to Jeremy, "I wish we were free like those squirrels out there. I don't like being locked up like this."

Jeremy appears shocked and replies, "What?! Out there?!" he peers uneasily through the fence, past an old rusty red tractor and out into the dark surrounding woods. "Are you out of your mind?! It is a big, treacherous place out there…it's no place for us chickens!" Yelps from a pack of coyotes echo off the walls of some far off canyon as if on queue, confirming for Jeremy what he is passionately trying to tell his foolish friend.

"Well," Ben says, "maybe not, but I just feel that there is so much more to do and to experience…it feels like we're just watching life go by."

Just then, a little iridescent flying creature appears from seemingly out of nowhere and stops to hover right above Ben and Jeremy. *"It's a fairy,"* whispers Jeremy. The two stand frozen, not knowing where this beautiful, strange and tiny creature has come from or how it is able to suspend in midair. It darts quickly back and forth from one spot to another, apparently examining them, just as they examine it. At one point it moves so quickly toward them that it seems to be aggressively diving at them.

"W-w-what do you want from us?" Ben says, uneasily.

The visitor finally speaks, "Why are you afraid?"

"What makes you think I'm afraid?" replies Ben.

"You stuttered," the visitor says.

"Well, you startled us," says Ben, defensively.

"Us?" queries the creature, rotating her head from side to side.

"Yeah, u-uh," Ben begins, looking around for his friend.

"There you go again!" she observes.

"Hey, what did you do with Jeremy? He was right here next to me! Are you one of those magical fairies I've been warned about?" interrogates Ben, trying to fit the little visitor into some chicken folklore box.

"No, I am not a fairy, I'm a *hummingbird*, and your friend just did what chickens do when they don't understand something…he ran and hid. I notice that you are still here," she says with amusement.

"I am curious," replies Ben. "Who are you?"

"My name is Crystal," she replies. "It is good to meet you, Ben."

"How do you know my name?" Ben asks, incredulously.

"Oh, lots of folks know who you are," replies Crystal with a smile.

"How do they know me?" Ben asks.

"Let's just say that you seem different from a lot of these chickens that you live with. You stand out," Crystal replies.

"Oh…" replies Ben, a bit self-consciously, still not understanding how she knows his name. "How do you float in the air like that?"

"I am not floating…my wings just beat so very quickly that they are difficult to see."

"Why do they beat so fast?" asks Ben with increasing fascination.

"Because they are small so they have to," the hummingbird explains.

"Why don't you have normal-sized wings like the other birds?" Ben continues, curiously.

"Say, you sure ask a lot of questions for a *chicken*!" she replies with a wink. "You know, I used to wonder that same thing when I was younger."

"Well, at least you can fly. I'm just a chicken stuck behind a fence, and I'm even envious of squirrels," says Ben, grumpily.

"Why be envious?" asks Crystal. "I used to be envious, too…wishing that I had larger wings like other birds, but as I got older, I just accepted that I was different. If I wanted to stay in the air, then I had to give one hundred percent, no matter what!"

The hummingbird demonstrates by stopping her wings and *falling*.

"No! No! Flap your wings! You'll hit the ground!" Ben screams.

Just before reaching the ground the hummingbird starts flapping her wings. She laughs and says, "Sorry that I scared you, but you see? I *have* to give one hundred percent no matter where I am or I can't choose somewhere else."

"I see…I sure wish I could fly. I'd give *anything* to fly!" declares Ben, even though his wing has healed enough that he is no longer wearing his straw sling.

Crystal thinks for a moment, and then says, "Well, should you miss experiencing this moment by spending it just wishing that you were somewhere else? Can you be grateful instead for where you are right now? The more you resist where you are, the harder it is to move forward. In order to move ahead, it helps if you can accept where you are in this moment. It's all about your perception. Does that make sense? Once you've accepted where you are in life, then the slightest shift in your perspective can put you somewhere completely different in no time at all." She demonstrates for Ben by flying all around him, flitting so quickly that it's a challenge to keep up with her. Then, as quickly as she had appeared, she was gone.

"But...wait! Don't go! How do I...?" Ben just stands where he is for a while, looking up at the patch of clear sky toward where his new little friend had just flown. At first he wonders where she has gone and if she will ever return. Ben thinks about everything she had just shared with him. He wonders what it means to change his perception.

A moment later, he looks away from the sky, peers through the fence to where the squirrels are playing. He glances down and sees an acorn lying amongst some straw and is inspired to reach for it. Picking it up by the stem with his beak, Ben tosses it into the air and begins to kick it around. He starts laughing and has a gleam in his eyes...he is *enjoying* himself. "Hey Jeremy!" he shouts and runs into the barn. The day is slowly fading into evening, and the sky turns a brilliant shade of orange, as a breeze rustles the leaves of a nearby lemon tree.

ACORNBALL

Days fly by, as Jeremy and Ben play their own version of acornball with the pigeons that live in the rafters of the barn. They play for hours, rain or shine, having fun. To Ben, acornball is more than just a game. It allows him to free his mind and put his full attention into something physical. Over time, acornball balloons into a major event for the barn, and takes on a life of its own. No longer the fun little game it started out to be, it is the main attraction in the yard, pulling everyone in as they all root for various teams. Life has become *exciting!*

"Start the game, already!" a blue jay shouts. It is the final game of the tournament between *The Squirrels* and *The Feathers*. The blue jay is accompanied by many chickens, crows, cardinals, pigeons, and various other birds, which have perched themselves upon the stack of tiered hay bales. A sparrow perches atop the barn to act as a lookout for Farmer Brown and his dog.

"My bet is on the hairy team!" one of the crows jeers, egging on Ben, Jeremy, and their team of pigeons, who are huddled up planning their strategy against The Squirrels.

"The losing team must confront the Egg-stealer!" another crow heckles, and an "Ooooooo!" flutters through the crowd. Laraine swoons and faints as other birds move to her aid, fanning her with their wings.

Humphrey chases the crows, and they fly to a higher row of hay. "I've had just about enough of the two of you!" he warns.

Ben glances up at the crows and then back down to his team and says, "Let's pretend the acorn is the Egg-stealer's head!"

"Yeah!" Jeremy and the pigeons reply with excitement.

A blackbird flies into the barnyard with an acorn, lands between the two teams, and calls out, *"Let's plaaay baaall!"* He drops the acorn to the ground and flies off to land on the wooden fence, where he can act as referee. Both teams rush for the acorn in their attempt to kick it.

Everything about acornball excites Ben, from going after the acorn, kicking it, picking it up, and running with it under his wing, the wind against his face and the air in his lungs, all the while dodging and avoiding the other team, and passing the acorn to his own team members.

Using his speed and large size, Ben plows into the squirrel that had reached the acorn first, and kicks the acorn past another squirrel to Jeremy, who scoops it up with his wing. Jeremy circles back around his teammates for defensive blocking. Being the charming show off that he is, Jeremy runs past some young cheering hens, gives them a wink, and dodges several squirrels that reach and paw for the acorn. He runs past a marker on the fence, scoring the first point for The Feathers. Cheers explode from most of the feathered crowd, but the crows are silent, as well as the squirrels on the fence beams, and those peeking their heads out from under the bottom rung. Jeremy does a little 'chicken dance' and he spikes the acorn, which bounces into a stack of hay. The ladies coo and swoon over Jeremy, the handsome young rooster.

"Yay, Jeremy!" his mother shouts from the stands. The other hens cluck noisily and giggle fitfully as Jeremy preens for them.

"There will be no gloating allowed!" blurts the blackbird, as he flies down from the fence to search for the acorn. He tosses straw here and there until he finds it. Picking up the acorn by the stem with his beak, he glares at Jeremy and returns it to the center of the "field" for another round.

With some fancy footwork and teamwork, The Squirrels are able to score a point shortly thereafter to tie the game. Both sides score several more points, and the blackbird calls the usual fouls. A couple of times, the sparrow had to whistle, and everyone ducked behind hay bales, flew off, or pretended that they were doing their normal activities. At last, the moment has come for Ben to show his true mettle. The game is tied and Ben decides to go for the winning point.

"Clark, over here!" shouts Ben to his teammate who has the acorn. Clark avoids several squirrels as he jumps into the air and flings the acorn to Ben. Jumping into the air, Ben catches the acorn in the fold of his wing.

"Drop it! Drop it!" the crows shout.

Ben feels exhilarated as he lands behind Jeremy, who offers himself as a barrier between the squirrels and his buddy.

"Get him!" a squirrel screams from the fence.

Acornball requires full commitment and focus. Ben feels like he is one with his body, the acorn, and the other players. There is no past or future, only the present moment. The squirrels are no match for Ben as he dashes and darts past and through them while they attempt to dislodge the acorn from the protection of his large wing. Ben jumps over two squirrels for the winning score and the crowd goes wild.

"Hooray for The Feathers!" cheers the crowd.

The crows and squirrels groan.

"Great job, Ben!" Etta shouts.

Ben grins at Etta, as Jeremy and the pigeons jump on him. Ben's heart is pounding. In these moments he doesn't care who he is, where he is, or even why. He just loves the sensations surging through his body as he plays this silly game that he and Jeremy call acornball.

~~~

That night, Ben settles onto some crunchy hay and replays the day's thrilling game of acornball in his mind. He eventually drifts off to sleep as cheers fade from his mind. It is one deathly quiet evening during a new moon. High above Farmer Brown's farm, a canopy of diamonds drapes against the black night sky. Ben is awakened by a noise. He peers around in the dark, but – even with his keen eyesight – it is difficult for him to see anything....

Ben listens carefully for a moment and hears some unsettling sounds coming from the far left corner of the barn. He strains to see through the chicken wire, but can only make out a black shape, which Jeremy had told him is the place from where the Egg-stealer comes. Ben notices that the eggs, which were left out, are now gone.

He jars Jeremy awake. Jeremy says groggily, "W-what is it?"

Ben whispers, *"Jer', the Egg-stealer is here!"*

"Y-yeah, so?" replies Jeremy, half asleep.

"So!?" exclaims Ben, "Don't you care?"

"It comes all the time," says Jeremy, yawning. "It's the agreement we have...you know that! Now can I go back to sleep?"

Grotesque slurping sounds echo from the hole. "Can you hear that? *This is not right!"* Ben says forcefully.

"I know!" replies Jeremy, "...but there's *nothing* I can do about it." He turns away from Ben, while stifling his feelings of guilt and shame.

"But there is!" counters Ben. "I want to help!"

"How? It's been coming for as long as I can remember!" says Jeremy, resigned.

"The past doesn't have to dictate the future!" Ben states firmly. "We can put an end to this, once and for all!" Ben glances around the nearly pitch black coop in the direction from where the sounds originated. He leaves the coop and walks forward in the dark toward the sounds. The sounds suddenly stop. Pigeons coo and flutter their wings high in the rafters.

"Ben, what are you doing?!" Jeremy asks, with concern in his voice.

Ben is too focused to acknowledge his friend's question. He inches toward the corner of the barn, where he hears a rustling noise outside, directly on the other side of the barn wall. Not finding an opening big enough to fit his large body through, he quickly runs past Jeremy, who is sticking his head out of the coop. Ben silently steps out of the barn, leaving Jeremy speechless.

The brave young eagle turns to his right and notices that a light is on inside Farmer Brown's house, shining brightly through a large window. The silhouette of a cat sits motionless in the window, and the old farmer walks by behind it. Ben ducks out of the light and turns to go the other way, for he doesn't want to be seen by the farmer, nor the dog.

He decides to take the long way around, and thus hurries along the barn's right side wall to the back and peaks his head around the corner. He can't detect much of anything except various dark shapes and shadows. Ben proceeds along the back wall of the barn with caution, while on the other side of the rear wall the pigs sniff and grunt at his feet through the wooden planks. He moves ahead, looking for anything unusual…but sees nothing, although he does have the unsettling feeling of being watched. The rusty old windmill creaks overhead as it spins slowly, and insects chirp here and there. A breeze moves its way through the grass outside the fence and reaches Ben, rustling his feathers, causing him to move his head sharply in that direction. Just then, he steps into a hole and loses his balance. Ben falls forward onto his chest, "Ouch!" he exclaims.

"Ben, is that you?" whispers Jeremy from the other side of the wall. "Are you okay?"

"Y-yeah, I'm fine," replies Ben with his eyes closed, "I just made a stupid step." He opens his eyes and sees two glowing red eyes glaring at him through the fence. "Hey you!" he shouts. Ray the dog is barking now from the doghouse. The eerie red eyes vanish into the tall grass and weeds. A horse whinnies nervously in the adjacent pasture.

Ben gets to his feet and stumbles to the fence, peeking through at black nothingness. "And don't come back!" he shouts, not even sure if those red eyes belong to the devil he is after. A while later, in the stillness, Ben becomes weary and his mind begins playing tricks on him – every shape and sound is the Egg-stealer, watching him…hunting him. He returns to the coop feeling kind of silly…like a failure. *What were you hoping to accomplish anyway?* he asks himself.

"Ben, what happened out there?!" asks Jeremy, obviously shaken.

"Oh, nothing," replies Ben. "I just tripped and fell on my face – it's very dark out there." Jeremy giggles. "It's not funny, Jeremy!" Ben snaps. "That monster is out there somewhere and we have to stop it!"

Jeremy is wide awake and beginning to get the full truth of Ben's argument. "What can we do?" asks Jeremy, hesitantly.

"I don't know," Ben replies, "but we will think of something."

"You two go to sleep!" Humphrey bellows from his resting place.

Jeremy is left in the darkness with his thoughts. If he challenges the Egg-stealer, then he is putting his family and fellow chickens at risk. If he *doesn't* do something, then he and the chickens have to live with the constant fear and guilt of giving up their eggs to this intimidator.

He is torn between these two choices, but he realizes deep in his soul that *now* is the time. With his brave new friend, the scales have tipped and the opportunity is at hand; for as a young rooster, he feels responsible for protecting his fellow chickens, and proving himself to be worthy of the duties of protector that will eventually be his.

He wants to make his father proud, but he is so scared. Nevertheless, he knows he must try – he must *face his fears*. Jeremy is clear that he has to do something, but it takes him a while to fall asleep that evening – he tosses and turns all night long as shadowy figures run through his mind and haunt his dreams.

STRANGE NOTIONS

For the next couple of weeks, Ben and Jeremy devise a plan for freeing the coop from the Egg-stealer's hold. They study the exact location and size of the hole from where the creature enters so that they have a better idea of what they are dealing with. The two of them also track how often the beast shows up – it does not appear every night but there seems to be a consistent pattern, as if the monster has a circuit and this henhouse is just one of many stops along that deplorable path. After much thought and planning, they come up with a fairly elaborate plan and they make the necessary preparations.

One day after much practice, Ben says excitedly to Jeremy, "So, are we ready, Jer'?"

"I think so," replies Jeremy, trying to match his friend's excitement and repress his nervousness at the same time.

"Good," continues Ben, "then it goes like this…" and Ben goes on to spell out their plan: "We wait until everyone is asleep, and then we quietly sneak outside of the coop to where the two eggs are left out for…"

"For that no-good, rotten murderer!" Jeremy interrupts.

"That's right," Ben agrees. "…for that no-good, rotten murderer. We hide the eggs behind a bale of hay where you and I will also hide and wait. We have to make sure we keep each other awake because we're not sure how late the thing will arrive."

"Oh, I'll stay awake for it alright. You can count on me, Ben!" declares Jeremy.

"Great," says Ben, happily. "When it arrives, I will jump out from our hiding place and block the hole so it can't escape."

"Can't I block the hole?" asks Jeremy. "I want to be the one to trap that monster!"

"No. I'm bigger than you, Jer'," answers Ben. "Besides, you have a very important job to do."

"Yeah, you're right!" says Jeremy enthusiastically. "I run outside to where we have hidden the acorn in the hay, and I fling it against that metal milk bucket to wake the dog."

"You got it!" affirms Ben. "And I'll chase the creature out of the barn."

"Yes," continues Jeremy, "while I hide around the corner of the barn door and jump out to scare it toward the direction of the dog!"

"Ha, ha!" laughs Ben. "Exactly, and since we have blocked the side of the barn with enough hay to stop a pig, it won't be able to go that way."

"Nope!" confirms Jeremy. "Then we both just chase it under the fence and the rest is history. It suffers the same fate as Laraine's sister...good riddance!"

They both touch wings in a bird handshake.

~~~

Humphrey looks on from a distance as Ben and Jeremy discuss their plans about stopping the Egg-stealer. Humphrey comments with suspicion to Jeremy's mother, "I don't trust him, and I don't like Jeremy spending all of his time with him – he's so different from the rest of us."

Humphrey continues, "I know you feel sorry for him and feel that we should open up our home to him, but he's filling Jeremy's head with all sorts of crazy notions. The other day, he was actually trying to convince Jeremy that he should try to fly! Can you imagine?" Humphrey asks, angrily, his feathers getting more and more ruffled. "I even caught them trying to jump off the old milk cow's bucket! Jeremy almost twisted his ankle!"

"There, there, dear, I'm sure it was harmless enough," Etta says soothingly.

"How can you say it was harmless? He almost broke his leg, I tell you!" the powerful old rooster squawks.

Etta persists, "Humphrey, I'm sure he wouldn't do anything too foolish, he's..."

"He's too much like your father!" bellows Humphrey, interrupting her. "I never liked him filling Jeremy's head with strange notions like: '*You can be anything you want to be*'…and now this!"

"But, dear, Jeremy loved his grandfather, and Dad would never let any harm come to Jeremy," Etta counters.

"He told Jeremy that the secret to living a full and free life is to *face his fears*!" the rooster says, bitterly. "How wise and protective is *that*? He was always going against 'the code.' Then there were those long talks with that spooky phantom, and, well, we know how that ended!" rants Humphrey, ruffling his feathers indignantly.

"Dad took great pleasure in those talks," Etta remarks, defensively. "I was concerned as well, but he said that there is no need to be afraid of the phantom. He said that it's just an owl, a bird like us, not a phantom at all. They used to have harmless philosophical discussions."

"Those philosophical discussions were the beginning of the end for him," Humphrey grumbles. "Besides, we have no business conversing with the flyers – we're not like them; it just leads to bitterness."

"Is that what you told Jeremy?!" Etta asks, shocked.

"Of course!" replies Humphrey, confidently. "He idolized your father. How else could I keep him from following in your father's footsteps?"

"My father died of old age, after living a full and productive life!" declares Etta. "I *want* Jeremy to follow in his footsteps!"

"Harrumph! We'll see," says Humphrey, as he watches his son playing with Ben. "We'll see..." Humphrey is hurt and angry at his wife's last statement. *Jeremy should follow in my footsteps! My rules will keep us alive!* he thinks to himself.

AN ANGEL

A large pinecone falls into the chicken yard next to Ben, startling him and interrupting his and Jeremy's conversation. He looks around and notices the scents and sounds of the blustery day. The sheep are bleating, and birds call to one another, as the wind wafts its way through the forest of trees, searching for anything it can lift and carry to some other location. It carries scents and pollen, leaves and seeds, even twigs and brittle tree branches. The wind circles Ben with the smell of dry hay. He prefers to be outside, as opposed to inside the barn where it reeks of damp straw, pig slop, and cooped up farm animals. The wind stirs something in Ben and reminds him of a simpler time – yet there is something about it that seems to taunt and challenge him. He looks up and sees a bird soaring high above the farm. He looks back down and notices the caterpillar's chrysalis, feels sad, and wonders what has become of his tiny philosophical friend.

Jeremy interrupts his reverie and tosses an acorn to him. They begin laughing and teasing one another. "You're looking more and more like a squirrel than ever, Jer'," Ben goads.

"Oh, yeah? Well, I've seen more amazing *crows* than you, Ben!" counters Jeremy. "You play acornball like a *sparrow*!"

Humphrey calls to Jeremy and tells him to go inside the barn.

A distant cry echoes in a far off valley as Ben looks through the fence, past several cows and bushy white sheep and the spinning windmill, at a range of lofty mountains in the distance. Ben feels wistful as he hears the cry of a bird and again longs for flight. He closes his eyes and dreams of soaring....

Humphrey walks up behind Ben, jarring him out of his daydream, and says to him sternly, "Listen, Ben, I don't know *who* you are or where you came from, but I think you're a bad influence on my son. I want you to stay away from him. Do you hear me?!"

Stunned, Ben replies somberly, "I don't know who I am or where I came from either; I'm just trying to figure that out. I didn't ask to be here...*Dad.*"

Humphrey then states firmly, "Well, you can figure that out on your own without involving Jeremy!" The rooster turns to leave, but then turns his head back without really looking at Ben, and adds coldly, "I am not your father!" Humphrey pompously struts away with his head up, and disappears into the barn.

Ben feels hurt and rejected, wondering who and where his real parents are and why they abandoned him in this lonely chicken yard. He looks out past the fence at nothing in particular while fighting back tears, which cause the landscape to appear like a watercolor painting.

~~~

Later that day, in the mid-afternoon, Ben overhears Humphrey, a group of chickens and some crows, clucking and cawing about him around the corner of the barn: "He's such an odd bird, not like us chickens at all!" "He's so quiet...he never has anything to say." "He's funny looking too! With those big eyes, his hooked beak and large feet. What kind of chicken is he anyway?" "The other day, I actually saw him eating a mouse!" "No...really?" "That's disgusting!" "Maybe *he's* the Egg-stealer!"

As Ben hears all of this, he begins to feel very sad, and then angry, especially at that last remark. Maybe they actually believe this! He feels as though hardly anyone loves or understands him. Jeremy and Etta try, and he appreciates their caring friendship, but he knows that he isn't like the other chickens. Ben feels that maybe they are right...perhaps he doesn't belong. He suddenly misses a place that he can't even remember. Ben notices a bird fly toward a distant mountain and he soberly sketches the scene in the dirt below his feet.

Just when he is feeling so lost and alone, a beautiful, dazzling, white blur lands on the fence near him. From Ben's perspective, it is blocking the sun's rays, which make it appear to be glowing like an angel. He is taken aback by its appearance. Ben had heard stories from the chickens about an enchanting white being, but he never thought he'd ever see one with his own eyes. He wonders if he should run inside the barn and hide.

"Hello there. Mind if I interrupt?" the visitor asks.

"Excuse me?" says Ben, a bit mystified.

"Do you mind if I interrupt...your wallowing in despair, that is?" the radiant one says, with humor in its voice.

"Are you one of those angels everyone talks about?" inquires Ben. The white being laughs indulgently. Feeling mocked again and not understanding this visitor's sense of humor, enchantment turns to defiant confrontation. Ben snaps, "Leave me alone!"

"Oh, come now," the visitor implores, "you can't mean that – you look rather alone right now and very unhappy about it. I am a dove, by the way, and my name is Belinda. Why are you so sad?"

"Well, I don't know how to *fit in*," admits Ben, feeling more and more dejected. "I try, but I'm not like the others. For one thing, I'm so hungry! I feel weak if I only eat the grain that they eat; I need something more. I don't look like them either. I just don't belong!"

"There, there…has it occurred to you that perhaps there's a grand reason for all of this?" Belinda asks.

"For being a *misfit*?" Ben inquires, bewildered.

"Perhaps your differences are your strengths!" Belinda suggests.

"Oh, I don't know…" Ben says, unconvinced.

"You really don't know how amazing you are, do you?" she asks.

"*Amazing?!* No, I don't!" Ben exclaims. He feels less amazing than ever right now, after Humphrey all but tossed him out of the yard.

"Well you *are*…all of us are!" proclaims the dove, lovingly. "The problem is that some of us forget, and then, well, we stop behaving in wonderful and amazing ways. You are *loveable* just as you are, you 'so misunderstood bird,' you!"

"Wow, I am *lovable*?" asks Ben. "Me?" His doubt settles in, even as his heart hungrily listens to this dove and her encouraging words.

"Of course you!" answers Belinda, "But, my friend, it's not so important what *others* think of you; how you think of *yourself* is much more important. If you want to be loved and accepted," Belinda pauses and leans toward Ben, "well, you must first love and accept yourself. What do you appreciate most about yourself?" inquires the dove.

Ben ponders this last question for a moment and then shares, "Well...I don't get scared very easily, and I love to learn. I also care about my friend, Jeremy. He and I love to play acornball, and we've gotten pretty good at it! I have a really active imagination too...although some of the others say that I daydream too much." Ben starts to feel a little better about himself, and even smiles at the thought of his daydreams. He can't quite imagine what his life would be like if he couldn't dream.

"Good! I daydream too, by the way," affirms Belinda with a wink. "Consider this: maybe there is something only *you* can give to the chickens." Ben thinks about this.

After a long pause, Belinda asks, "Do you know why the other birds can fly?"

"Why?" Ben asks with peaked interest.

"Because they take themselves lightly!" the dove laughs joyfully, and then coos a loving good-bye. She leaves Ben alone with his thoughts, although now he isn't feeling quite as lonely and sorry for himself as he was before she visited.

He watches her as she flies away toward the sun and over some tall wild mountain roses growing a short distance beyond the fence. The sunlight shines through the rose petals, imparting a vibrant white magenta.

THE PLAN

Humphrey's words still sting Ben. He thinks to himself, *I like being here with Jeremy, but now I have no choice but to stay away...unless I can make a difference here.* Ben thinks about his and Jeremy's plan to stop the Egg-stealer and how this would improve life in the yard, and make Humphrey feel more accepting of him. He trusts that their plan will create the harmony that the chicken yard has been lacking.

Ben holds his head high and starts to walk proudly back to the barn. He passes the two crows who have always enjoyed teasing him. One crow caws at him, "Hey Ben, we just heard about your most recent friends!"

Ben stops and asks, "Oh, yeah? W*ho*?"

The other crow responds, "Some mice that were just in time for supper!" The crows laugh.

Ben adds, "Yeah, and they tasted like crow!" They all laugh together, but then the crows stop and look at each other. Ben walks away and says, "You guys are funny, we'll have to do this more often – you guys are some piece of work!" He chuckles to himself. The crows just stare at Ben and then nervously glance at each other, rather baffled, not getting the reaction they expected from him.

As Ben walks into the barn, Etta approaches him and says, "Ben, I understand that Humphrey had some unkind things to say to you."

Ben remembers how sad he felt a while ago, before Belinda's visit, and asks, "Why is he so mad at me?"

Etta responds, soothingly, "He isn't *mad* at you, dear. What you need to understand is that he feels a great responsibility to protect all of us. Humphrey has been very upset that we have lost so many of our eggs to the Egg-stealer, and that he hasn't been able to do anything about it." Etta confides, "Besides, Humphrey has been very busy and tired from chasing all of the mice away, which come to eat our grain; although he has mentioned to me on several occasions that these raiders of our food have not been coming around nearly as often as they used to." She looks directly at Ben.

He looks away and then back at Etta, and then down, and says unconvincingly, "Really? Well, that's odd. I wonder why that is?" Ben kicks the dirt and watches the cloud of dust drift off.

Etta smiles and continues, "Please don't take what he said personally; he is truly trying so hard to be the best that he can be. Sometimes he just sees anything or anyone who is different as a threat to our safety."

"I know that I'm different," Ben shares with Etta. "I don't know why...I try to fit in, but everything I do just seems to broadcast that I'm some sort of *alien*."

Etta says, "Ben, I've been watching you and how you are with Jeremy...you are a true friend and companion to him. He was very lonely before you came. His grandfather was his best friend and Jeremy took his passing very hard. You've brought a new spark into his life, and you have such a unique way of looking at the world. I've truly enjoyed watching both of you play and hearing the two of you talk and I can tell that Jeremy is very happy."

"But Humphrey told me to stay away from Jeremy," Ben says, with disappointment in his voice.

"I will talk to him, Ben," promises Etta, "but remember that he is doing his best to find his way, as we all are. I just want to thank you for being who you are – our little world here is better because of you. Don't ever try to be someone or something that you're not – you are unique and perfect just as you are." Etta gives him a big hug and then hurries off to check on her chicks.

A warm glow starts to grow in Ben's chest as he whispers to himself, *"I am perfect just as I am...."*

~~~

Later, as the day's light begins to wane and becomes twilight, dark and ominous thunderclouds begin to gather in the east and Ben sneaks behind the barn. He begins to pace and ponder as he mulls over the coming night. A pigeon lands on the fence next to him and asks, "What's going on, Ben? It looks like something is troubling you."

"Oh, hey, Norris," Ben replies, "I need to speak with Jeremy, but Humphrey wants me to keep my distance."

"Why's that?" questions Norris.

"It's a long story," says Ben, looking around the corner.

"I'll get him for you," volunteers Norris, as he flies off toward the front of the barn. "Are we on for acornball, tomorrow, if it isn't raining too hard, that is?"

"Uh…yeah, sure," says Ben, with acornball being the last thing on his mind.

Jeremy shows up a short time later and asks, "What's up, Ben? It's time to go inside; Dad says a storm is coming. What are you doing back here…and why did you send Norris to get me?"

"Your dad wants me to stay away from you," answers Ben.

"What?! Why?!" exclaims Jeremy.

"Ssshhh!" whispers Ben, *"he'll hear you…besides, there isn't much time!"*

"Time for *what*?" asks Jeremy, "Ben…you're scaring me."

In the distance, Humphrey calls for Jeremy.

Jeremy turns his head to look back as Ben continues, "I think tonight is the night to stop the Egg-stealer!" As Ben said this, it surprised even himself, but he knew that it was time. Based on their previous calculations the beast is due back on the next full moon, which Ben knows will rise tonight. Besides, Farmer Brown is sure to notice him one of these days, since he has been checking the coop more often as the chickens had feared. Ray is also barking more frequently around the barnyard, sensing a maturing eagle in the chickens' midst. Ben doesn't know that he is an eagle, but he has always known that he's been concealed from the giant for a reason. Now is definitely the time to confront the Egg-stealer, for Ben may not get another chance.

Grasping Ben's conviction, Jeremy slowly turns back toward Ben, with fear growing in his eyes, but he calmly nods and states, "Okay, Ben."

They both touch wings in a bird handshake, as Humphrey calls again, "Jeremy!"

Jeremy says, "I have to go," as he turns to leave.

"We can do this!" Ben calls after him. "Just remember the plan."

"I know!" says Jeremy, running toward the barn entrance.

Ben watches Jeremy run off, and then slowly follows him back to the barn.

"Who, who, who..." echoes in the dusk air.

~~~

Back at Benjamin's home, Alexander and Claire slowly unroll the gift from Candor, and they both stare at it again. Putting his wing around Claire, Alexander says reassuringly, "He'll return to us, Claire."

"Yes, I know," Claire agrees quietly, "I believe in him."

Benjamin's brother and sister stop by, exhausted, excited, and out of breath. They reach their parents' nest, and are barely able to get out cryptic words between breaths, "It's about Benjamin!" Dolores begins.

"We just heard from a turkey vulture, who heard from a sparrow, who heard from Aloysius, who..." Delmar adds.

"...who overheard that Benjamin is planning on challenging some creature tonight...which has been terrorizing the chickens!" Dolores finishes.

Alexander drops his end of the scroll, turns to Claire and says, "You see, Claire? We have to intervene!"

"Now hold on, dear," counters Claire, "I'm just as concerned as you are, but you heard Candor."

"Candor, Shmandor – this is our son down there!" Alexander exclaims.

"This is a turning point for him, dear," comforts Claire, passionately. "Remember, he is *your* son...he will be fine. We have to let him have this rite of passage!"

Alexander takes a deep breath and looks out toward the farm. Noticing storm clouds that have gathered to the southeast, he closes his eyes and nods. He feels what every parent feels when their child reaches this point in their development. It is a rite of passage for the parents as well: a kind of surrender, to resist helping their child, because they know that the time has come for their child to make his own way. As painful as it is to face the possibility that their child could fail, he knows that he must allow his son to grow into the leader he was born to be.

Alexander sends a silent prayer and blessing to Benjamin and opens his eyes. He turns to Claire and smiles with a smile so tender that it breaks her heart. He says with mixed emotions, "Of course, I know that he has to do this on his own. I just feel helpless and proud and frightened, and yet confident that our son will come through this. How is it possible to feel all of these conflicting things at once? I believe in him, too, and I am so proud of him!"

THE EGG-STEALER!

That evening, just after sunset, as the full moon peeks through the advancing storm clouds above the horizon, two young hens each slowly and somberly roll their eggs outside of the coop as their offering to the Egg-stealer. With tears in their eyes, the young mothers know that it is a sacrifice they must make for the good and safety of the rest of the coop.

On this night, the tide is about to turn, because Ben is too impatient with the constant level of fear in the yard. He and Jeremy have decided to take a stand. They watch the hens in their solemn ritual of sacrifice. They wait until everyone is asleep, and then they quietly sneak out of the coop and stow the two eggs in a safe, warm and dry area of hay behind the hay bale where Ben and Jeremy will also be hiding.

Jeremy is well aware that he is stepping outside of the 'Safe Code of Conduct for Chickens.' His parents, and quite possibly the whole coop, could shun him – or worse – for his disobedience. It is the price he is willing to pay, for he is no longer willing to sit idly by and allow fear to be his dictator.

Ben and Jeremy are determined not to fall asleep. Their hearts are pounding so hard! They hide behind the hay bale near the Egg-stealer's hole, ready to catch the creature by surprise and chase it past the coop, and then out into the yard where Ray the dog will catch it.

After some time passes, however, they both begin to doze off. The wind has been moaning louder outside, causing the windmill to creak and spin rapidly. The chicken coop is very still and dimly lit, and not a creature is stirring nearby, except an occasional cow lowing in the pasture.

On the verge of sleep, Ben notices movement out of the corner of his keen eye. He has not experienced this level of fear since...well, since a time in his distant past before this chicken coop, before meeting Jeremy. Ben pictures himself for a moment on the edge of a high precipice, looking down into a very deep void. He knows not what dangers dwell down there, and he experiences a strange and terrifying feeling of falling!

Ben has no idea what lurks in the shadows of the chicken coop, but he senses it closing in. He imagines that this very well could be his last night alive. He fears for his life, and for his dear friend Jeremy's. In that moment, however, Ben catches hold of his mind and thinks, *I don't have to think about the worst thing that can happen. I need to focus on what I want.* He closes his eyes and gulps, accepting his destiny. He opens his eyes wide and peers into the darkness before him....

A form begins to appear against the wall, low to the floor of the barn. The shape starts out very small in the corner and then grows larger. Instantly, Ben's senses bring him to full alert and he turns to Jeremy, who has long since fallen asleep and is peacefully snoring.

"Jeremy, wake up," Ben whispers. *"Jeremy, hey Jer', it's here!"* The ghostly shadow moves mysteriously back and forth, resembling a flickering black flame, as the creature

sniffs the air for some tender morsels…for now, two eggs will do. The dark figure stops abruptly as it realizes that not all of its feathered hosts are asleep.

Jeremy finally awakens, groggily, "Um, huh, what?" The slithery shadow splits in two, with one part going toward the coop and the other coming directly toward Jeremy and Ben! Fear grips Ben as he realizes that the plan is falling apart – Jeremy is still half asleep, and this thing appears to have duplicated itself, and has picked up on their hiding place.

Nevertheless, plan or no plan, Ben becomes very aware of two things: one, that no matter what, he will not allow any eggs to be taken; and two, he feels extremely protective of this new family of his. Ben realizes that despite the fact that they have had their differences, he cares about the chickens very much.

Perhaps your differences are your strengths!

Ben rallies Jeremy and they run after the creature that has now crept inside the coop searching for eggs, while the figure coming toward them divides once again into two smaller distinct forms.

"Mom!" Jeremy calls to his mother who is incubating her egg. "Mom!"

Etta wakes up and sees a dark shape moving quickly toward her. She screams and runs away just as the large Egg-stealer lunges at her, taking a bite out of the space that had just a moment ago been occupied by her body. A huge gust of wind breaks the latch on the barn window and the shutters smash open!

The intruder, which is really after the eggs, isn't upset at all to find one resting unprotected in Etta's nest! Quickly, the nasty thief grabs the egg, exits the coop and runs past Ben and Jeremy back toward the hole from whence it came. Ben and Jeremy pursue it, and Ben bites down hard on the creature's tail, stopping its forward movement and causing the egg to fly from its grasp, straight toward the hole!

Jeremy leaps for it and stops the egg just before it falls into the hole. "Ben, I got it!" shouts Jeremy, as he tucks the egg under his wing.

"Not for long!" hisses one of the smaller Egg-stealers, which had been advancing on Jeremy. It snatches the egg from Jeremy's possession, as its partner in crime slams Jeremy against the wall.

Meanwhile, the head Egg-stealer, who is quite perturbed that Ben had bitten its tail, turns to snap at him. "Don't you know that it's impolite to bite your guests?" it growls angrily.

Ben quickly releases its tail and jumps backward to barely escape being bitten. "You weren't invited!" declares Ben, as he runs to Jeremy's defense.

"Are you okay, Jer'?"

"Y-yeah," he responds dazed, "but the egg isn't!"

By this time, the other chickens have been awakened by the turmoil and they are huddling together, not quite sure what to do. They cluck and shriek and make an awful noise. They would like to help out, but they are too afraid to confront one Egg-stealer, much less three! The chickens remain inside the coop where they feel safer with Humphrey's protection.

Ben runs after the bandit that now has the egg, but just as he reaches it the creature tosses the egg to its twin. They are happily playing keep away, tossing the egg haphazardly back and forth.

I must give one hundred percent, no matter what!

Ben jumps high into the air to catch the egg in the fold of his wing and amazes everyone in the process.

"Wow! Did you see how high he jumped?!" one of the chickens gasps. The rest of the chickens cluck and go on about Ben's leap, and squawk about the Egg-stealers.

As Ben begins to land, one of the Egg-stealers tackles him hard and the egg flies from his protective grasp, sending it airborne once again. Paws and wings combine in a frantic fury as the egg is tipped up and sails through the air toward the barn wall!

Jeremy dashes for the egg, stepping on a creature's head in the process as he leaps and catches the egg just before it would have smashed against the wall. Jeremy is quite pleased with himself and begins to do his acornball, goal-scoring 'chicken dance.'

"Ben, are you alright?" Jeremy calls out, remembering that Ben had been knocked down. The two twin Egg-stealers are closing in on Ben to get him out of the picture completely. "Uh, Ben?!" Jeremy's voice cracks.

Ben is quite stunned…he doesn't remember being jarred like this since a day in his distant past, just beyond his wall of recall. That event had traumatized Ben to the point of amnesia, but being slammed by the Egg-stealer has loosened something from within his memory. He has been winded, and his head and wing ache, as lightning flashes outside…and he remembers…*there was wind all around me, surrounding me, roaring in my ears, and I was lost and frightened and fighting to get back…to get back to where?…to get back home! And then it happened…I saw the gray wall of the craggy mountain rushing toward me and…SLAM! Then falling, falling, falling!* It is all starting to come back to him…and now he hears Jeremy calling. Ben comes to and says weakly, "Y-yeah…uh huh…I just need to catch my breath…" Just as Ben is about to be attacked, Jeremy's father emerges from the coop and blocks the advancements of the invaders. He fights them off with fury, pecking madly at the Egg-stealers, as thunder rumbles off in the distance.

Just outside the coop and peering in, the largest robber is scanning the entire area for other accessible eggs but has set its sights back on the one currently in Jeremy's possession. Jeremy runs from it while racing by the crowd of cheering chickens on the other side of the chicken wire. The Egg-stealer lunges at him! Jeremy is faster, however, and it crashes into the wall of chicken wire. Laraine pecks aggressively through the wire at the Egg-stealer. "You murdered my sister!" she screams.

Ray, the golden retriever, is awakened by all of the clamor and begins to bark. His barks are getting closer and closer to the heat of the action in the barn.

Jeremy once again breaks into his chicken dance. The chickens cheer, and Jeremy, forgetting that he's holding an egg and not an acorn, almost spikes it! The crowd suddenly goes silent…but Jeremy stops mid-spike and sheepishly gives the egg to his mother. As the chickens celebrate, an ominous dark and angry shape of the head Egg-stealer looms up, coming toward Jeremy who is cornered. The creature is done playing. It fixes its piercing red eyes on Jeremy and bears its sharp teeth. Now it has vengeance on its mind!

Ben is dashing to Jeremy's aid, when the two other Egg-stealers, leaving Humphrey wounded and gasping, now both rush toward Ben. The barn door slams shut while the shutters of the barn window are swinging open and banging shut in the tempestuous wind, and rain droplets blow through the opening like hot breath on a cold night.

Ben realizes that he is about to be crushed by the two Egg-stealers that are rushing toward him. He had never really worked through his trauma from the mountain fall. It had been repressed and forgotten, the price of which had imprisoned him in a world of fear, doubt and false identity, but now he is remembering. As his past comes rushing in, his head is reeling and his body starts to shake, but amongst the chaos Ben makes a conscious choice to forgive himself for his first flight failure, and thus break through this block once and for all and liberate himself from the shackles chaining him to the ground. "ENOUGH!" he shrieks.

Go within, Benjamin. Reclaim your power!

He closes his eyes and begins to feel an intense tingling sensation, almost like an electric volt of energy, surging through his body. His mind flashes on the past several months of living with this new family of his: the frustration of feeling like a misfit, of sensing that he has some great purpose but not knowing what it is. All of this happens in a matter of moments. He feels a culmination of every lesson that he has learned while living in this barn, and he knows that he has not come this far to be injured or worse by these creatures!

Your wings, sweetheart, spread your wings!

Despite all of the fear and pain coming up for Ben, he embraces it and then transforms it...and with every ounce of strength that he can muster, Benjamin channels all of his energy, opens his eyes, spreads his powerful wings, and begins to flap them until he is airborne!

Everyone is shocked! "He's *flying!*" "Look!" "But chickens can't fly!"

Benjamin can hardly believe it himself. It feels very surreal...and time seems to have stopped. He is a little nervous at not having his feet firmly planted on the ground, but he mostly feels exhilarated...for he *is* actually flying!

The two twin Egg-stealers crash into each other in their attempt to crush him. Benjamin looks down and sees the large Egg-stealer lunge at Jeremy with its sharp claws and teeth. "You chickens still haven't learned...from now on, we will need *three* eggs!" it hisses.

Benjamin locks his penetrating eyes on the beast and swoops down to grab it with his talons, right as it is about to mortally wound Jeremy. Benjamin continues to flap his wings and, lo and behold, he lifts the Egg-stealer higher and higher into the air.

Unexpectedly, the barn door flies open and in the doorway stands Farmer Brown holding a rifle. He is wearing a dark hooded raincoat which is dripping with rainwater, and he is scanning the entire barn with the beam from a flashlight, as a lighthouse would sweep over a tumultuous sea; he is a true giant to the chickens. His loyal dog Ray is next to him, barking excitedly. "What's all this commotion about? Weasels!" exclaims Farmer Brown. The twin brother and sister weasels run from them toward the chicken coop in a last-ditch effort to snatch an unattended egg left out during the scuffle; but the chickens, with newfound courage and in a united front, force the weasels to scurry back down the hole.

"What the...what's an *eagle* doing in here?!" the kind-hearted farmer exclaims while looking up to see Benjamin flying toward the open barn window, carrying the mother weasel, who is squirming to get free but more and more reluctant to free herself the higher they get. "Well, my friend, it looks as though you have things under control here...thank you," Farmer Brown says, as he leaves to fetch his shovel to fill the hole in the ground.

The chickens are left alone to settle things in their own way. They are very excited! "An *eagle*?!" "We've heard of eagles but we've never seen one up close." "Ben, you're an eagle!" they shout up to him.

Benjamin has other things on his mind. He notices from high above the scene of the battle that Humphrey is injured and needs help. Benjamin calls to the chickens,

"Take care of Humphrey!" The chickens quickly attend to Humphrey who is lying in some hay.

With more wing flapping, Benjamin rises higher and higher, up and up through the open barn window. The chickens watch him disappear and are left alone, feeling amazed and quite humble. Those who had made fun of Ben because he is different feel particularly ashamed. "Of course he is *different*! He's an eagle, the grandest of all birds, and he was living here with *us*! We've been blessed all of this time and we didn't even know it!"

Benjamin carries the Mama Weasel outside into the rain and wind, and feels tremendously powerful. He realizes in that moment that he can determine the weasel's fate of life or death right then and there, whether out of anger, revenge, justice, or simply because he can. For a brief moment, however, he locks eyes with the mother weasel. In her eyes he sees both love and fear; her love for her two babies, and the fear that she won't be able to provide for them.

Although Benjamin can see the beautiful aspects of the weasel, he also recognizes that she had resorted to intimidation and fear tactics when she had discovered the chicken coop and had begun preying upon the defenseless chickens. He recalls when he had mentioned to Jeremy that if someone hates it is only because one is afraid. He can see that now in the pleading eyes of the mother weasel. She was afraid for her young ones, and so she behaved hatefully, robbing the chickens of their eggs, and even killing one of the hens in the process. Benjamin understood the mother weasel because he himself killed and ate mice, but he felt that the weasels had crossed some invisible line, creating a climate and culture of fear amongst the chickens.

Benjamin realizes in that moment that his presence in the chickens' lives has rebalanced the scales, and will force the weasels to find food elsewhere. He feels compassion for the mother weasel and puts her down outside the fence, warning her, "Don't ever return here!" She is trembling with fear from the flight, and after a few moments of being motionless, turns toward Benjamin, hisses at him through her sharp teeth, and then scurries off to retrieve her children from behind the barn.

Benjamin flaps his wings and rises like a phoenix high above the barn and trees. He feels reborn! The storm, which had been raging throughout the night, has turned south away from the farm as quickly as it had come. Benjamin can see for miles as the full moon peaks through the remaining storm clouds, clearly illuminating the landscape. He hadn't realized that Farmer Brown has such an extensive farm. There are acres and acres of crops spread out over rolling hills. There are lingering gusts of wind from the storm that try to catch Benjamin and take him where they will, but he is very strong and agile tonight and he instinctively works with the wind, rather than choosing to fight against it. He allows himself to soar for a while over the encircling vast forest.

A tingling feeling fills his chest as he realizes that he is actually *flying*! Having been cooped up for so long with the chickens, he is now acutely aware of the vastness of space surrounding him and his own distinct freedom. Benjamin breathes in a deep breath of air, holds it, and exhales. He soars through the night, with only a few stars and planets visible through the clouds in the moonlit sky, and smiles as distant memories begin to flood his mind.

"Who, who, who are you?" Benjamin hears beneath him.

He looks down to see Aloysius perched on the top of a tall redwood tree. "Aloysius!" Benjamin calls down. "I'm discovering that, but I can tell you who I'm *not*!" as he makes a wide arc and circles the owl with joy in his heart.

~~~

Back at the barn, Farmer Brown has already filled in the weasels' hole and has plans to fix the barn window. "What's an eagle doing in my chicken coop?" he mumbles to himself, as he picks up his lantern and walks back to the house while calling for his canine companion, who is barking through the fence at the mama weasel, "Ray, come on, boy! We've had enough excitement for one night!"

Farmer Brown decides to fix the barn window in the morning, since it is too dark, damp, and dangerous to be climbing around on a ladder. He is pretty doggone tired to boot, from a long day of work on the farm. He is willing to take his chances with that eagle, because for some strange reason he feels like it is some sort of protector. Inexplicably, he trusts deep down that his chickens are safe. *How strange*, he thinks to himself over and over again.

The chickens are more than safe – they are jubilant: "Did you see how we stood up to those nasty, shadowy, weasel-Egg-stealers!" "They won't try anything else with us!" "Our future children are safe!"

A short while later, Benjamin flies in through the barn window. "Benjamin, you can fly!" announces Jeremy, reminding Benjamin that his dream has come true.

"Yes, I can!" states Benjamin, joyfully. The flight out of the barn has sparked memories for him of a place high up in the air...*home*. "But how is Humphrey?" asks Benjamin, concerned.

The chickens step aside to reveal Humphrey, who is propped up against the side of a hay bale. His head and wing are bandaged with some straw, but he smiles at Benjamin and gives him a wink. "I always knew there was something different about you, Benjamin!" he says weakly. Ben grins at him.

Benjamin, remembering that he and Jeremy had hidden two eggs from the Egg-stealer, tells the young hens where they are and helps to retrieve them. The chickens and the eagle settle in for the rest of the night, with the knowledge that this is probably the last evening they will spend together. They dance, sing, and celebrate throughout the night. Chickens and eagle...unlikely friends.

FAREWELL

With the first hint of morning, as the sky begins to turn a lighter shade of blue and then more golden pink, the chickens and eagle awaken.

Although they did not get much sleep last night, the whole coop is abuzz with energy. Benjamin walks outside to fill his lungs with air and the knowledge that he is free. He looks around and sees the yard one last time. The blue hazy mountains in the distance are calling him, but for now he takes in the sights of the only home he can clearly remember. Rain droplets glisten and drip off of the trees and the scent of pine fills the air, while the sun's rays illuminate the silk of the caterpillar's empty cocoon.

~~~

"Dad, don't do it!" Jeremy pleads.

"Son, it's my job, it's one of the reasons I'm here," Jeremy's bandaged father replies.

"But if you crow, Farmer Brown will wake up and then...well, we'll never see Benjamin again!" Jeremy sadly realizes.

"Jeremy, my son, you *will* see him again, off in the distance doing what he was born to do. He doesn't belong here anymore; he has a different destiny than you. Son, you are a rooster, you were born to carry on in my tradition and your grandfathers' before me. We are here to guard the chickens, to make sure that nothing happens to them. I'm very proud of you…the way you stood up to the weasels last night. It might soon be time for me to retire and for you to take my place," Humphrey divulges.

"Really!" says Jeremy excitedly, his chest filling with a glowing, warm sense of worth.

"Yes, really – you're just about ready to do what you were born to do," the father rooster says.

"No, Dad. Not yet! Let's say goodbye first," Jeremy begs. Jeremy helps his father walk over to the others who have now circled around Benjamin. He is exchanging goodbyes with each and every one.

Humphrey walks up to Benjamin and says kindly, "Benjamin, I want to thank you for what you have done for my family."

Benjamin responds modestly, "Don't mention it, Humphrey; I'd do it all over again. Besides, I want to thank *you* for being there for me against those weasels last night." Benjamin gestures to Humphrey's bandages and asks, "How badly are you hurt?"

"Oh, just a few scratches. I'd do it again, too," the rooster says, trying his best to hide the pain behind a tender smile. He pauses and adds, "I also want to say that I am sorry for what I said to you before. I should have been much more understanding and hospitable toward you."

"Forget it," Benjamin says. "You took me into your home, for which I am very grateful. You were just looking out for your family."

Humphrey closes his eyes and looks down, respectfully. He opens them and they touch their wings together. "It's funny," Humphrey discloses, pulling Benjamin aside, "I have never told anyone this, but before you arrived, I would often stare up at the windmill, as it spun in the wind day after day, and I would wish that the Egg-stealer would go away and leave us alone. I believe in some way that you are the answer to that wish. I mean, what are the chances of an eagle landing in Farmer Brown's chicken yard? Do you think I'm crazy, Ben?"

"No, I don't think you're crazy, Humphrey," Benjamin replies. "I can now recall days, as a very young eagle, when I would daydream about having an adventure like this."

"And all this time I was trying to push you away," says Humphrey, regretfully.

"We were both resisting what we wanted all along," Benjamin says, trying to ease Humphrey's guilt. "What we wished for was right before us and we didn't even know it!"

"I guess what we want doesn't always come the way we imagine, eh, Ben?" Humphrey asks.

Ben turns his head up toward the squeaking old windmill and answers, "Indeed, Humphrey, life is funny that way."

Before Benjamin turns to leave, Humphrey peers directly into his eyes and says sincerely, "Benjamin, I'd be honored to have you call me 'Dad'…and I will always think of you as my son."

Benjamin's eyes water and he smiles at Humphrey while saying, "Sure thing, Dad; it would be an honor. Take care of yourself and our family." Humphrey nods.

Benjamin moves over to Jeremy's mother and they embrace. "Bye, Mom. Thanks for believing in me," Benjamin tells her.

Tears filling her eyes, Etta clucks, "We've been so blessed to have you with us, dear!"

Benjamin turns toward Jeremy to say goodbye, "Hey, we really showed those weasels, didn't we?!"

"We sure did," Jeremy says, fighting back tears. "It looks like those hours of playing acornball really paid off. Benjamin, you're the best friend I've ever..." his throat starts to choke his words.

"Yeah, you are too," Benjamin replies. "I'll miss you, Jer'! Hey, but you've got some important stuff to do here!" he says, waving his wing at the entire group.

"Well, you can *fly*!" Jeremy says, smiling, as they hug.

"I'll always remember you," Benjamin says, and Jeremy nods in agreement.

Just then, Etta's egg, which had been the object of so much attention last night, starts to shake. It suddenly cracks open and out pops the fuzzy head of one dizzy young chick. They look at the new addition to their family, and at each other, and they all burst into laughter!

Benjamin bids farewell to all of the chickens and begins to flap his powerful wings and raise his body higher and higher, until he disappears with one last, "See you around; I'll be keeping an eye on you!"

~~~

That day, and from that day forward, a different voice crowed Farmer Brown awake…a younger, yet very capable rooster.

REUNION

Benjamin looks down at a pasture and sees a pair of horses running together. Sparrows and other birds chirp and sing as if in a symphony of celebration. As Benjamin rises higher and higher with every beat of his powerful wings, he sees the world from a new perspective. A beautiful, multi-colored butterfly flutters by, and he turns to look at the graceful creature just as it directs its gaze at him.

"Thanks for not eating me," the butterfly laughs.

"The little, green caterpillar!" Benjamin blurts, surprised. "Wow, you sure have changed! I can't believe my eyes. How did this happen? It's like…magic! The last time that I saw you, you were all wrapped up. I was wondering what happened to you."

"I know!" the butterfly shouts. "I had this awful nightmare that my own body was trying to kill me! I was really terrified, but I kept imagining and trusting that I was destined to survive, and become someone different and less limited than I had been. I had to let go of who I was in order to become who I am!"

Benjamin replies, "That was obviously no nightmare or imagining but something that was really happening…I mean, look at you!"

"Isn't it amazing?!" blurts the butterfly while giggling, unable to control its laughter.

"It is!" agrees Ben. "Let's fly!!!"

They fly together for a spell. Well, Benjamin actually flies circles around his multi-colored friend.

"I told you I had a purpose!" adds the butterfly.

"Wow! You sure did," replies Benjamin. "You are impressive, I must say!"

"You too!" responds the butterfly. "It looks like your purpose is unfolding for you as well!"

"So it would seem," Benjamin confirms. "It looks like we both have a similar one. Farewell, my friend."

"Good bye. Have fun flying!" the butterfly calls back, gleefully, as they both fly off in opposite directions.

~~~

Benjamin flies toward the rising sun where the sky is clear, except for some scattered white and gray clouds. Rays of sunlight burst through the clouds; while behind him in the distance a light rain refracts the sun's light, creating a beautiful rainbow arc. It is a glorious juxtaposition of weather on this perfect day, when everything is more vibrant and aligns in splendid harmony.

A whole new world has opened up to the young eagle. He glides through a deep canyon, over a rushing river and past a raging waterfall. With a slight shift of his wings he turns upward and flies over the dense pine forest. He lets out a loud shriek and the smaller animals in earshot duck for cover. Benjamin can see snow-capped mountains, an abundance of streams, lush valleys, and sparkling lakes below. *I had no idea what I was missing!* he thinks to himself.

He soars and thinks of his time with the chickens and of the fact that he thought he was one of them, *how silly! I'm sure glad I chose flight over being right about being a chicken!* Benjamin ponders everything that he learned from those he had met – the chickens, caterpillar, owl, hummingbird, dove…and even the crows and weasels. He understands that he never would have learned to truly know and accept himself, and to appreciate who he is, had he not had this difficult but enlightening adventure. *Who…who…who…would he be?* A sudden smile lights up his face. For just as a diamond is formed by heat and pressure, so was Benjamin's strength and beauty forged by the challenges and struggles that he overcame. Benjamin realizes that who he is isn't a chicken or even an eagle – he is something much more infinite than a kind of bird – he somehow feels like he is a part of everything and everyone, not separate…but connected.

Suddenly, a wonderful warm thermal wind lifts him even higher. Benjamin starts to recognize some nearby cliffs above the clouds. Just then he sees her; she is graceful and free, blissfully gliding along by herself. He realizes that something else had been missing in his life, but he did not know that it was absent until he saw her.

"Hi," he says, slipping alongside of her.

"Hello there," she says, surprised by her sudden companion, yet pleased by his boldness. She glances at him. He seems strangely familiar and also strangely strange. *Who is he?* she wonders. *There is something different about him. He seems innocent, yet like a hero, as if he has discovered some new land or has just saved someone. What is it about him? I like him.*

"Have you missed me?" he asks slyly.

"Yes. Where have you been?" she plays along, hoping to uncover his mystery.

"My name is Benjamin."

"I'm Brianna." They fly and soar together toward the cliffs, becoming instant friends.

~~~

Claire and Alexander are alone in their nest, having a quiet moment together. "Will Benjamin ever get through this ordeal, Alexander? I miss him so!" Claire proclaims.

"Of course he will," Alexander responds, comforting his wife. Alexander embraces Claire and closes his eyes. He wonders silently how his son fared through the night and if what he just told his wife is true.

When he opens his eyes, he sees a confident young male eagle land on a tree limb near their nest, along with a charming female companion. "Benjamin?" asks Alexander, blinking.

Claire quickly opens her eyes and turns around. "*Benjamin?*" she asks, not believing her eyes. "Benjamin!" she cries. "It's you! Oh, Benjamin!"

They all embrace with tears of joy in their eyes. "We've missed you so much!" says Claire.

"I know, but I was fine, really," Benjamin replies. His sudden flood of memories of his earliest days moves him. Seeing his real mother and father makes him choke up, but he does not want Brianna to see him like that.

"What happened?" asks his father.

"It's a long story," Benjamin continues, "and I'll tell you all about it in a little while, but right now I want you to meet someone. Mom, Dad, this is Brianna."

"Pleased to meet you," Brianna says.

"Welcome!" Benjamin's parents say to Brianna with open wings.

"Benjamin, your brother and sister have both gone off to build their nests. They are over on the eastern face of the cliff," Claire shares.

Alexander reaches for the scroll next to him and passes it to Benjamin. "By the way, son, Candor gave this to us while you were away," he reveals.

Gazing at his parents, and then darting a glance toward Brianna, he extends his talons toward the scroll and takes it from his father. *Candor!* Benjamin recalls the mysterious bird he had seen in so many of his dreams. He carefully unrolls it, not sure what to expect. His eyes widen as he looks over the scroll, in a state of disbelief.

After a short while, Brianna breaks the silence, "What is it, Benjamin?"

Benjamin just stands there, motionless, holding the scroll carefully with his sharp talons. He finally responds, "It's a drawing I carved for Candor when I was very young. He was tutoring my siblings and me, while my parents were both off gathering trout far inland. I barely remember anything back then, but this is very vivid."

"Are you both hungry?" Alexander asks. "We can have some salmon while you tell us all about your adventure. We were so worried!"

Their son responds assuredly, "It was all perfect, trust me." Benjamin looks back down at the etching on the scroll as he goes on to explain his story with the chickens....

VOWS

Several years pass as Benjamin and Brianna grow in their love, friendship, and understanding of each other. By this time, their white crowns are now almost fully developed. During a visit with their wise condor friend, Benjamin shares, "Candor, Brianna and I feel that it is time for us to bind ourselves to one another."

"How do you know, young ones?" Candor inquires, looking at both of them.

They exchange a glance and, searching for the answer, Benjamin replies, "We love each other unconditionally. I can't imagine my life without her. I barely remember a time when she wasn't a part of it," Benjamin asserts with great feeling.

"Of course, Candor, we both know that Benjamin hasn't always had the best memory!" Brianna teases as she winks at him.

Seeing them gaze at each other, Candor immediately recognizes a most profound and unconditional love. He smiles and looks up at the clear starry night sky and then turns to his young eagle friends and affirms, "I agree...the time has come for you both to commit your lives to one another. I can't imagine two souls more perfect for one another!"

~~~

In the near future, gathered together with their families, friends, and one very wise old condor to officiate, Benjamin and Brianna each exchange their vows with one another within a ring of pine needles and rose petals on the ledge of a cliff, overlooking the breathtaking valley and shimmering lake below. The couple's crowns, now fully developed, are shining brilliantly in the sunlight.

As Candor pronounces them husband and wife, he adds, "...and when the time comes to teach your babies to fly, please make sure that it is on a *clear* day!" Candor winks at Benjamin, and then at Claire. She smiles and looks at Alexander standing next to her, and he smiles back at her. She has finally forgiven herself completely for losing Benjamin, for she has fully accepted that it was the perfect path for her son.

Benjamin looks out at the loved ones who are witnesses to this joyful day. He smiles as he notices the assembled guests: his parents, brother and sister, Brianna's family and friends, Aloysius the owl, Belinda the dove, Crystal the hummingbird, who has remained unusually still during the ceremony, and a gorgeous butterfly.

The butterfly, however, is actually a descendant of Benjamin's friend, for just as the caterpillar's body had transformed into a butterfly, so did the butterfly's body transform into a being even more beautiful, albeit in some unseen realm – a bright and peaceful version of Jeremy's dark netherworld; speaking of which, Aloysius reassured Jeremy that his grandfather had also gone to the brighter place, and that the owl himself had nothing to do with the old rooster's passing! Benjamin can feel the spirit of his little friend through the butterfly's presence and they smile at each other.

The other guests each smile at him in acknowledgement of how far he has come, and of the new adventure that is about to begin. As Benjamin is noticing those who are gathered, he experiences a small pang of sadness as he realizes how much he wishes that his friend, Jeremy, and the chickens could be there. He would like to share this day with them, and so he vows to drop a rose and an acorn onto the haystack for his chicken family.

Although the chickens cannot attend, Aloysius had been kind enough to inform them of the ceremony so that they could participate in their own way. On this special day, all of them have gathered in the yard to honor the eagle who had made such a difference in their lives. Some of the braver chickens decided to jump up onto the stack of hay bales, while Jeremy made it to the very top where his eagle friend liked to go to be alone. *It feels right, you should try it, Jeremy*, the young rooster recalled a week ago and as a result he summoned his courage during the week and gradually worked his way up to the top, with his parents nervously watching on. Benjamin's chicken family looks on toward the mountain in remembrance, along with reverence and gratitude for their eagle friend. Even the crows are present on the roof of the barn...surprisingly silent. The thoughtful owl also vowed to share the ceremony details with Jeremy upon his next nightly visit to the barn.

Benjamin reflects for a moment about his journey and how everyone along the path was a part of his awakening. His friend, the little green caterpillar, sparked a sense of greater purpose in him. Aloysius taught him to question his limiting beliefs about himself. Most importantly, he learned that he creates his reality based on what he focuses on. Crystal taught him to accept and be grateful for where he is in life in order to choose and create something different, and he embraced the power that occurs from full commitment. From Belinda, he learned to truly love himself and then to share that love with others – by giving unconditionally of himself, Benjamin received so much! He nods back to them in appreciation for their gifts to him, and silently vows to honor them by passing on their wise counsel.

After the ceremony, Benjamin and Brianna say their goodbyes to their guests. Lastly, Benjamin walks over to Candor and from under his wing he pulls out the scroll and passes it to the condor, saying, "I believe this belongs to you, my dear friend."

The old condor takes the scroll and, looking directly into Benjamin's big golden eyes, says with a grin, "We may need to set aside some time to explore this gift of yours." They touch wings and embrace.

Benjamin and Brianna fly away toward the gorgeous sunset, while Alexander steps into the ring of pine needles and rose petals next to Candor. Claire converses with Belinda, Crystal, and the other guests. All of them watch the two young happily married eagles fly off together.

Looking forward without moving, in a very regal pose, Alexander asks his wise friend, "Why do we forget, Candor?"

The old hunched condor turns one eye up toward the large eagle, and looking back at Benjamin and Brianna now soaring high over the majestic lake, pauses, and then calmly replies, "So we can remember..."

Alexander looks down at the scroll, while stating very matter-of-factly, "You know, Candor, before Benjamin had that adventure, I would have sworn that was just an image of a mountain and the sun, or possibly a star, but now..." he pauses, "well, now I am pretty convinced that it is one of those human-built wind contraptions, although how would he have known?" Carved onto the piece of bark is a simple sketch of a tall triangle, with several intersecting lines located at the top corner of the triangle.

Candor just shrugs his shoulders, while looking back up at Benjamin and Brianna, and with an aloof demeanor casually adds, "It could be anything." He steals a glance from Alexander.

The eagle and condor look at each other and after a long pause they can't contain themselves any longer so they both burst into hearty laughter. Alexander places his large wing around Candor, while looking up at the recently married couple, who are just about ready to begin an ancient eagle ritual.

~~~

Benjamin and Brianna fly as high as they can above the clouds, where they clasp talons and begin to spiral in an exhilaratingly dangerous freefall, as eagles have done since the beginning of time. They are as close as two birds can be while flying…falling, feeling each other's hearts beating faster and faster, until just before meeting the lake's glassy surface, they spread their wings and fly off to find a nice sturdy place to build their nest…leaving behind a lake of endless ripples….

~~~

In time, Benjamin has become a father; he is flying in search of food for his new family. After catching a fish, he comes to rest on a branch of a large oak tree, not far from Jeremy's home. In the tree, several branches over, there are two chicken hawks in intent conversation.

"Did you see that farm we passed over? I'll bet there are chickens there!" one of the chicken hawks says to the other.

"Let's go back to see. I'm hungry!" the other responds.

Suddenly, a loud and thunderous "NO!" startles them both! Benjamin swoops down and lands next to the branch that they are perched upon. "You'll have *me* to answer to if you even *think* about going near that farm!" he bellows as he lifts himself up into the air with his powerful wings and shakes the dead fish at them.

The two chicken hawks quickly fly off, getting as far away from Benjamin as possible; neither one of them wants *anything* to do with upsetting that mighty eagle!

It feels good to protect the chickens, even though he had heard from Belinda the other day that *Jeremy* had done a brave job of protecting the chickens and their eggs, by chasing a large egg-eating snake out of the barn. Benjamin is very proud of his friend, knowing that he is a courageous protector.

He looks on toward the farm and that rusty old windmill, barely turning in the still air, and sees Jeremy teaching some young chickens how to play acornball – although recently, Crystal had told him that the chickens had renamed it 'Save the Egg.' She also shared that Jeremy, Jenny and the younger hens – using Benjamin's hay bale technique – can even fly for short distances, even though Humphrey, the older hens and Farmer Brown, are not too thrilled about this new development. Benjamin smiles to himself as he notices that Jeremy is really having fun.

Benjamin flies home to his mate and children, filled with a sense of pride and esteem.

~~~

Sometime later, a young eagle couple is telling a story to their three young babies: "…and so in the end, children, it wasn't Benjamin's size, his or Jeremy's skills from playing acornball, their bravery, definitely not their elaborate plan, or even Benjamin's ability to fly that saved the chickens and their eggs from the weasels that fateful night, for the creatures could have come back.

"Even if Benjamin would have killed the mother weasel, which he easily could have done with a quick thrust from one of his rear talons, her children escaped, and they surely would have had their own babies…coupled with the fact that they would have been very angry and bitter as a result of losing their mother. The chances are very likely that the children and their descendants would have come back again and again, and not just for eggs…but for revenge. I doubt if even Farmer Brown and his dog Ray would have been able to fend them off forever.

"No, children, it was Benjamin's love and compassion that ultimately saved the chickens and their eggs. When he locked eyes with the mother weasel and spared her life, she was forever transformed in that moment, never to return again. So it was not fear alone that kept her and her descendants away for good.

"Benjamin was a very wise eagle, and remember, he never would have had the opportunity to help the chickens if he hadn't forgotten and then remembered who he was. We don't always know how life will unfold, but nevertheless…everything that happens has a purpose," the mother eagle concludes.

"Who is Benjamin?" the eldest baby asks.

"Well, actually, he *was* your great, great grandfather, who lived in the days of the old mystic, Candor," replies the father eagle.

"Candor! Really?" the young eagle gasps.

"That's right," affirms the mother eagle. "And now, it is time for all of you to learn the one thing that distinguishes us from most other creatures living on Earth."

"You mean...?" the oldest eaglet replies, with an air of tentative anticipation.

"Yes," interjects the father. "It is time for your first flight!"

"Hooray!" all of the eaglets shout with joy.

"I want to be like Benjamin!" the oldest eaglet declares.

"And I want to be like Candor!" adds the next oldest while waving his wings to symbolize some mysterious hocus-pocus.

"Well I want to be like Jeremy!" blurts the youngest.

"But Jeremy couldn't fly, silly," preaches the middle child. "This will be one short flight for you!" he laughs.

"Yeah, I know...but he was a good friend to Benjamin," counters the bold little eagle, thinking back to the young eagle and rooster playing together on the farm.

"That is true," the father agrees. "Besides, who knows what the future holds for chickens. It was taught by the ancients that all of us birds descended from groundlings."

"No! That can't be true! We are eagles…the grandest of all birds!" the oldest protests while sticking out his chest with pride, and his brothers nod in agreement.

"Now, now," says the mother eagle, "let us show a little humility. Whatever the case may be, what do you say that we just be ourselves, the best we can?"

"We can definitely learn from our predecessors and carry on their legacies, all right?" adds the father.

"All right!" the three eaglets agree.

"Wonderful," says the mother. "So are we ready?"

All three nod in agreement, nervously, and trembling with an innate fear of falling, the three young eagles are one by one gently pushed from the nest by Mom and Dad, "Remember…claim your power!" One by one they *fly*. It is a beautiful day, the sky is a brilliant blue, the air is calm and clear…not a cloud in sight.

Acknowledgements

This book would never have been completed without the consistent, gentle nudging of the father of this project. When the challenges of life have encroached, William has always kept his eye on the prize. He has been the primary editor, spending countless hours combing over the pages, time and time again, adding his inspired personal touches. Thank you, love, for your vision and tireless encouragement. I can hear the eagles' call!

There are many who have been in the wings through the years, who have continued to encourage us and lend their expertise, feedback, inspiration and love. We are so grateful for our family of friends, which includes our family. Thanks to my brother, Ken Marschall, for his beautiful vision for our cover art. Thank you, Ken, for being a shining example of successful creativity. Many thanks to our daughter, Brianna, William's parents, Dolores and John, William's brother, Joseph, and William's sister-in-law, Suzanne, for their input, feedback and encouragement.

Thank you to my brother, Bruce Marschall, for being my creative champion so many years ago. Thanks to Kathy Benson and Harvey Cohen for their inspiration and wisdom. Thank you to Scott Austin and Phil Mendez for their enthusiasm. We appreciate my sister, Kat Lilore, for giving so freely of her time, expertise, and for her fresh eyes and fine-tooth comb, and to our brother-in-law, Jo Lilore, for his expert web advice. Thank you to Nikki Russo and Jeanette Roknian for their wonderful applause. Thanks to Christia Crocker Karp, for 'lighting up' – we look forward to what the future holds!

Thanks to Diana Franklin, Lisa Schneiderman, and Laurie Quintero for always being such great sources of encouragement. A special thank you to Mrs. Helga Schindler, our adopted aunt, who has always been an inspiration to us, as well as a supportive friend. To Marlee Nelson, my baby sis ~ thank you, Marlee, for always being there to remind us that our dreams are worth it!

Thanks to my long time friend, Michael Graziano, whose lovely inspiring words have always warmed my heart. Thank you, Michael, for referring us to Henry Hutton, whose expertise in the world of publishing has given our baby the wings to fly! Thanks also to Elmore Hammes, for his attention to detail while formatting the book.

They say that when raising children, it takes a village. Well, in many ways, "Wings" is our child. We finally realized that every writer must surrender to their editor…that we were just too close to the project to be completely objective and that the time had come for us to bring in another set of eyes. We just didn't realize that the credit for the editor would expand to more than one.

First of all, we would like to thank Holly Mae Howard. Just when we thought we were complete and ready to go to print, Holly inspired us to write four more chapters! Aside from William, Holly is our primary editor and we deeply appreciate her tenacity and advocacy for "more Candor!" We would, however, be remiss if we didn't also thank the following people for their feedback and input in the final days before publishing this revision. A great big thanks to my talented nephew, Shane Stranahan, our brother, Joseph Hicks, our dear friends, Jeanette Rocknian and Nikki Russo, and a very special thank you to our sisters: Marlee Nelson for her wonderful editing skills and beautiful prologue which she was inspired to write; and Kat Lilore, who once again brought her keen eagle eyes to "Wings."

Lastly, gratitude is due to all whom, by their willingness to shine, have directly or indirectly touched and inspired us throughout our lives.

About The Authors

Elizabeth Emily Hicks and *William Raymond Hicks,* both natives of Southern California, are a husband and wife team who met through a transformational workshop environment. During much personal growth together, Elizabeth, a.k.a. Elise, and William were inspired to write *Wings, The Journey Home.* Elise and William are both students of history, psychology, self-empowerment, and quantum physics. Their intention is to teach what they have learned in a fun and inspiring way. *'Wings'* is their first published book, and they are working on several other books, including a book of poems, short stories, and musings.

Made in the USA
Lexington, KY
26 June 2011